POTATO

Possibilities of Time and Things Overthere

Published June 2020
©Doppler Effect
Dopplereffect.org

*Dedicated to Archie Gent.
Baby brother and sunshine of my life.
Everything is possible.*

ABOUT DOPPLER EFFECT

Doppler was created in 2015 by our founder, Danielle Morgan (aka PF Flumpton).

After working as a 'jack of all trades' marketeer for British start-ups and iconic for 20 years.

Danielle decided to make a change.

Inspired by David Bowie, mindfulness, Brene Brown and the time it takes to write a sci-fi novel, she found herself re-connected to creativity, to a community and to a lifestyle she loves.

Ultimately, this is what Doppler is *all* about.

We want EVERYONE to have the opportunity to reconnect with their creativity and their calling.

We are here to help creators make a living doing what they love, to take a step out, live ambitiously, and to know that the life they want is ***never*** out of reach.

When people are free to live creative, more fulfilling, meaningful lives the world will be a better place.

We are changing the world for the better.

People **need** this.

This is for **everyone**.

And the time is **now.**

THE DOPPLER EFFECT EXISTS TO HELP CREATORS MAKE A LIVING DOING WHAT THEY LOVE.

DOPPLEREFFECT.ORG

@HELLODOPPLER

Table of contents

Prelude

Chapter 1. Overthere

Chapter 2. Polly & the 'friendly' badge man

Chapter 3. Donald gets kidnapped

Chapter 4. Introducing Bert

Chapter 5. Polly makes a plan

Chapter 6. Tony and the doctor

Chapter 7. Polly & Bert unite

Chapter 8. Dr Matlock & Dr Andreas Cardolp

Chapter 9. Teatime theme time

Chapter 10. The search for Donald

Chapter 11. They know where you live

Chapter 12. Public appeal

Chapter 13. Polly & Bert meet the officials

Chapter 14. Madagascar

Chapter 15. Donald's secret mission

Chapter 16. The lost night

Chapter 17. Bye-bye Bert

Chapter 18. Bye-bye Donald

Chapter 19. The Mentor Tome

Chapter 20. Love codes life

Chapter 21. Polly goes to Overthere

Chapter 22. Tony cleans up

Prelude

Have you ever wondered, what will the world look like when we are introduced to our intergalactic neighbours?

On the planet Earth, in its 1.986543 millionth year, shortly after its birthday, the momentous event arrived. Overthere made 'first' contact.

Finally, we could answer the question.

Are we alone?

No.

Of course not.

Chapter 1. Overthere

NASA was as surprised as anyone when the satellite Supkin was intercepted and the first message from Overthere was received on Earth.

Charlie Broadbean, NASA administrator, practically choked on his cornflakes while listening to the alien missive disrupt the otherwise soothing tunes of HotJams radio. He rose to his feet and shouted 'Shit!' several times, startling his poor dog Smudge so much that he immediately deposited his rectal response on the kitchen floor.

It dawned on him, as he listened intently and mopped up the mess, that he was going to be bloody busy from now until the end of his lifetime.

A surprise in a long line of surprises.

The received communication from Overthere was of impeccable quality and spoken in 6,500 different Earth languages. It was well beyond lunchtime the following day before the welcome message was fully transmitted, for many in the Northern Hemisphere it was reminiscent of listening to the results of Eurovision Song Contest to be read out, only less tedious.

The first Overthere weekly bulletin, as heard in its English translation, read as follows:

> The suns are shining.

> Contentment to the human race.
> We are the people of Overthere.
> We embrace you with love and sanity.
> Welcome to the Alphafarag.
> You are never alone.

Speculation and suspicion ensue.

After the initial message, there was radio silence for two weeks. Then came the regular weekly broadcast, consisting of intermittent facts and numbers about the Alphafarag and Overthere. The transmission was an attempt to get Earth up to speed with the cosmos.

Overthere's welcome caused Earth's media to go into overdrive and eventually caused the press to self-implode. There were multiple reports of journalists catching fire and disappearing all over the world. Alas, no one believed or indeed cared if the stories were true.

For most people, very little changed in their lives. Having spent decades hearing sensational news, there was little they could do, other than carry on and wait to see how things turned out.

According to statistics, an uplift in divorces and a rise in unemployment took on unprecedented new heights. Zealous religious groups professing the end of the Earth sprung up, but it was difficult to judge if these were new groups or just the same old ne'er-do-wells.

A self-professed genius, and former bass player of an ageing rock band, speculated that the people of Overthere had already visited Earth without anyone knowing. He went on to insist he'd known about this all along and had even written several successful songs to warn everyone. At first, nobody paid much attention. He was, after all, reasonably irrelevant in modern times. It was when he started turning up at parties wearing only a machine gun as underpants and yelling 'The aliens will kill us all!' that he was considered dangerous. His subsequent arrest, re-emergence to fame as the leader of the Anti-Alien Task Force and eventual execution, marked a prophecy for darker times to come.

Arguably, the best development as a result of the alien contact was the creation of International Welcome Day. Governments all over the world recognised an excellent PR opportunity when they saw one and granted everyone a day off work. Millions of people took to the streets with banners and welcome mats to wave up at the sky and celebrate the 'discovery' of second life. Offers of food were sent up into the ether, sellotaped to drones and helium balloons. New songs were created and sung by out of tune children at the tops of their voices. At least that's how it began.

The year International Welcome Day was created, all was good. Earth was starting to get a handle on things. Not much else occurred in the second year, other than several civil wars continued, a moron invented time travel and a fake digital currency collapsed. But by and large, everything was relatively OK.

Perhaps it is worth adding a little more context at this stage. Describing everything as 'OK' is maybe painting too merry a picture of Earth's ever-developing inferiority complex. Already feeling a little out of touch, intelligent life on Earth, collectively speaking, had no idea that Overthere existed and had believed for thousands of years that it was the only thing worth talking about in the universe. If Earth were a person, you might call them self-obsessed, with little or no awareness of anyone around them. Having had its eyes forced open to the fact it was no longer top dog, intelligent life on Earth felt minuscule and insignificant. As a result, it started to overcompensate.

Academics and members of the public entered spirited debates around the nature of life on Overthere. As most popular fiction would have it, aliens were synonymous with invasions and always resulted in a battle to the death. After years of conditioning and a tendency for violence, it was challenging to dissuade humans from fearing such an attack.

During years three, four and five, things started to get interesting. If you were observing a pub fight, these years were the moment when 'things got tasty'. Which loosely translates as time to abandon one's pint and get the hell out of there. Unfortunately, though the population was up for leaving this metaphorical pub, there was no way out. So, everyone remained stuck on Earth.

During years six and seven, things took a turn for the worse. Speculation of alien spies and alien witch-hunts were on the rise.

It was generally understood and agreed that no one knew what was going on. If knowledge is power and power is money, governments were bankrupt and rich and powerful people the world over became weak, leaving the poor increasingly desperate to take control. Conversely, this excited the hoi polloi, who had long had it rough and were, not so secretly, delighted at the prospect of new owners.

Thankfully, not everyone believed that an invasion was on the cards. For example, a peculiar group of people from Stoke on Trent in England wondered if a recently deceased pop star, who had written global hit songs about being visited by people from outer space, was an alien and made several requests for an autopsy. Two women from Burgas in Bulgaria also stumbled upon the real motivation for Overthere's contact with Earth. They even went so far as to write a book about it. Alas, with the ever-declining human desire to read, sadly no one looked at it aside from the authors and their mums.

Chapter 2. Polly & the 'friendly' badge man

It had just passed 10 pm and there's a knock at Polly's door. This strikes Polly as odd for several reasons. Firstly, she lives on the third floor; usually, the buzzer would sound before a knock. Secondly, she lives in London and it's a Tuesday; no one ever pops round on the off chance. And, thirdly, Polly had just been thinking about how people never pop round on the off chance anymore.

Not being the most safety-conscious person in the world and, despite the lateness of the hour, she hurried to her door shouting, 'On my way!'

As she approached the door, a name springs into her head, and with it a connection to whom the late-night caller may be.

Bert.

If anyone in the whole world could be responsible for a late-night knock at the door, it would be, without doubt, something to do with Bert.

Bert had that utterly fabulous quality of never being somewhere when you want him and being everywhere when you don't. Polly hadn't seen her brother in over ten years and, seeing as he had never met any of her friends, she often wondered if Bert existed at all. Even his name sounds silly enough to be made up. Then again, so did hers. She had often wondered who in their right mind takes a look at a small bundle of life, not a day upon the Earth, and decides 'Polly' or 'Bert' as a suitable alias to carry around with them for the next 90-odd years.

Polly often damned her parents and their sense of humour, or lack thereof. Then guilt kicked in, since they had both died some moons ago.

Assuming he does exist, Bert is Polly's brother. His age is unknown, mainly as Polly can't remember exactly and Bert wasn't one to keep track. In truth, most details of Bert are relatively hazy.

'Hello?' floated the sound of a distinctly male voice through her front door.

'Ah, hello,' she replied, opening the door.

There in front of her stood an unfamiliar and yet, in Polly's immediate opinion, a friendly-looking man, who is not Bert. At a glance, he was significantly taller than Polly and wearing a jacket with a little yellow badge on it saying 'Friendly'.

'I'm sorry if it strikes you as odd, knocking at your door at such an ungodly hour,' said the friendly badge man.

'No, not at all,' said Polly. This is weird, she thought.

'Someone let me into the building downstairs, so I came straight up,' he beamed at her.

'Ah right,' nodded Polly.

Why is it that some people do not seem to mind leaving a bit of silence in a conversation? Polly thought. She had many friends that seemed happy with these sorts of circumstances, but not our Polly. Her natural response was to fill the void with sound, regardless as to if it made any sense, which it most certainly never did. Polly started to feel awkward on behalf of the stranger on her doorstep.

'Well this is awkward...umm...so, how can I help?' she said smiling.

'I'm sorry. I should explain myself,' he replied. 'You must think I'm some kind of crazy murderer.'

'No, not at all,' Polly said, which was quite the opposite of what she was thinking.

Now the reality was starting to kick in. Polly is stood in her doorway, door wide open, in nothing but a Power Rangers T-shirt (it's not hers, but this isn't the point) and some jogging bottoms. It's late at night, and there's a tall man that she doesn't know standing in front of her. She could see it now in future press releases: 'Missing: a young woman from Putney. She was last seen in a Power Rangers T-shirt.'

'My name is Donald,' the friendly badge man said.

What a ridiculous name, Polly thought.

'I'm not stopping,' he continued. 'I've come on behalf of your brother Bert. He gave me a key to get in the front door.'

'Hang on. I thought you said someone let you in?' said Polly, immediately suspicious.

'Well, yes I did. But I thought if I told you straight off that I'd let myself in, you may have been a bit wary and then asked lots of questions, which I don't have time for.' Donald tapped his big foot nervously.

'Yes, you're right, this way is far better. I wouldn't have thought of that,' Polly replied drily.

'I have to pass you this code,' said Donald, in a tone that told Polly her previous sarcasm had been lost on him. 'This code,' he continued, 'holds the key to everything. Please listen when I say that this code will bring you whatever it is you desire. It holds an infinite amount of power.'

'OK, right,' said Polly, accepting the folded piece of paper.

'I know this all seems a bit bewildering and don't feel at liberty to do anything if you don't wish to. Throw it away you can. It is a beautiful universe we have; one that holds choice.'

'OK.' Polly didn't know what else to say to that.

'I must leave now, but you can ask me two questions before I go.'

'Two questions?' repeated Polly.

'Yes.'

'That wasn't one of them used up, was it?'

'No, I'm not a genie.'

'No of course not, because *that* would be ridiculous,' sneered Polly.

'Please hurry,' asked Donald, looking uncomfortable.

Polly's mind raced for a question. She must ask this looney something useful as she knew it was something to do with Bert. What was he playing at? She must think quickly.

'Umm…why is it written on paper?'

'What?'

'Why is it written on paper?' continued Polly, with what she thought was a confident manner.

He gave her a perplexed look. 'I'm not sure I understand.'

'Well, I mean…this password.'

'Code,' corrected Donald.

'What?'

'It's a code, not a password.'

'Oh, yes. Sorry.' Polly tried again, 'This code holds all this power and stuff.'

'Key to everything. This code holds the key to everything and will bring you whatever it is you desire. It holds infinite amounts of power.'

'Sorry, yes, that. So why is it on a piece of paper? It seems strange. Why is it not on something more futuristic, like a' Polly cast around for an example. 'Like a USB stick or something?'

There was a long pause as Donald looked at her unblinking. 'This is what troubles you the most?' he asked.

'Well not the *most* but it seemed as good a start as any.'

'Well, it just is. This is how it's being communicated to you…by the medium of paper.'

'Oh, OK.'

'Is it some kind of special paper? Unbreakable paper or invisible paper?' Polly continued.

'No, it's just paper; A4 in size,' Donald offered.

'Ah, OK.' Polly tried to give him the impression that the information was useful.

'I must say, your questions are not what I expected. Maybe this is why you've been passed the code. But I must leave now. I'm sorry to have caused you any inconvenience.'

'No, not at all. My pleasure.' Polly engaged the smile she reserved for charity collectors and her boss.

'Goodnight Ms Polly.'

'Um. Goodbye then, Donald.'

Only 23 humans in the entire world had knowingly met an alien.

Approximately 18 Earth-months after the first publicised contact from Overthere, the invitation of the millennia arrived over the airways. Overthere invited Earth to visit.

This very first meeting was a cause of great embarrassment to Earth and had somehow, by way of a blessing, remained relatively unknown or conveniently forgotten over time.

Naturally, there was a lot of excitement at the time and a whole heap of logistics to sort. If you thought it was a pain in the arse trying to get to your mate's house in Bethnal Green on a Sunday during a public transport strike, then you need to alter your perspective considerably.

The plan was to meet on the Moon. Knowing of Earth's limited skill set for space travel, Overthere sensitively chose a destination that would provide a sense of common ground for Earth, and its eager yet fragile sense of achievement. For everyone involved on Earth, it was the most exciting thing to happen since the initial contact itself. Everything, from the invite turning up to having to pack fresh socks and buy miniature space toiletries, was all anyone could talk about for months. With every angle analysed, every moment anticipated, the flush of a budding young romance flourished in all but the hardest of hearts.

Earth had a date.

Seven astronauts were carefully selected from each continent – four women and three men – with trillions and trillions of global donations. It was a genuinely touching moment to watch great nations unite in this common goal. The magnificent seven were selected in the most meticulous and gruelling way. They were young, primed and ready to represent. The entire recruitment process occurred with somewhat of a dreamlike quality. Never in human history had the planet come together with such elegance, precision and drive. It was as if the entire future of humanity depended on it.

On the morning of the 25th of November, as the selected few set off, the whole globe tuned in to watch the event, with people openly weeping in the streets with pride.

The meeting itself was described afterwards, by the seven members still capable of articulating it, as the closest feeling to the divine they had ever experienced. Sadly, all the recording equipment cut out moments before the moon landing took place, leaving many baffled and fuming. Needless to say, no one was particularly happy about having to rely on the drawings.

With this oversight representing the pinnacle of all that was wrong with Earth, British publications such as UK Today had a field day. There was a follow-up article about an inevitable alien invasion and how most Brits did not want aliens coming over here taking all our jobs.

Interestingly, UK Today is more pertinent to Polly than she realises. The very day the alien invasion article was published, there was, for the first time in the history of the tabloid, a fascinating and vital article by one Donald Pigeon (friendly badge man).

In short, it wasn't Polly's fault that she couldn't pick an alien out of a line-up, but she was reasonably sure that, if she had met an alien, they would probably look a bit like Donald.

Here stood this 27-year old woman-child, dumbstruck and looking at a, now closed, front door. Her mind engaged in what we imagine to be a state of steady evaluation and reflection, but, more accurately, was a painfully slow reconnecting of events.

Did that just happen? Echoed over and over in Polly's mind.

After what felt like ice ages, but was perhaps only several minutes, Polly suddenly leapt into action. Throwing on her mock polar bear slippers, she wrenched open the door and flung herself down the stairwell. If she was quick enough, she might just catch up with him.

Bursting out into the chilly night, Polly looked all around her, including up at the inky black sky. Quite why she checked the sky, she wasn't sure. Perhaps to see if he *was* an alien (and he did look a bit alien-like) flying back to his spaceship. Could aliens fly? It was anyone's guess.

Speed walking to the end of her street, she stole a look down the road leading to the common. It was unusually cold for January and, seeing as global warming had yet again failed to deliver the promised tropical winter to the British Isles, this wasn't all that surprising.

There were a few people out and about still – there was a couple wandering around looking lost, one man in a cape and a girl teetering along clutching what looked like some sort of kebab, probably from the Van of Death on the corner. Other than the standard late-night scraps of people, there was nothing of any great interest, only the standard leafy landscape of west London, and certainly no sky-scraping potential aliens.

Polly decided to head back to her flat, feeling stupid and far more aware of her appearance than she was when she'd left less than five minutes ago. I'm going to get myself a nice cup of tea and have a little think about all of this, she thought to herself as she shuffled indoors to the warm glow of her flat. Putting the kettle on, she reached up for her favourite chai blend and went to open the fridge.

Damn. No milk.

And she'd forgotten to ask after Bert too.

Chapter 3. Donald gets kidnapped

Donald had not vanished. Instead, he had simply walked out onto the street and locked himself into the nearest public toilet. These gravity-induced panic attacks were awful. Entirely how life had survived on this planet, given the level four gravity pressure, he'd never know.

After several minutes, he ventured out from his hidey-hole and onto the small green outside. Still feeling anxious, he looked around him, did three roley-poleys and instantly felt better. He hadn't intended to dash off so quickly, so no wonder the poor girl was somewhat baffled.

He was just as clueless about his reasons for being here. It wasn't so much that he disliked being on Earth. Despite the air pressure problems, pollution, rampant violence and the obsession with temperature, it was an immensely beautiful place. He longed, however, to explain to someone, anyone at all, that it was all a bit 'alien' to him.

This was no place to waste time preying on his thoughts. Donald jolted into action and walked towards what felt like the way back to the tube station. As he approached the heath, he paused and looked up. He was reminded of how remote this place was, with only the Moon for company. The Moon had bewildered Donald when he first arrived as he'd never seen anything quite like it. He didn't like the way it just loitered there in the sky at night. He felt like it was watching him. No, he didn't like it one bit - stupid Moon.

People of the Earth seemed to feel very passionately about the great lump of shining rock in the sky; poems, films and love songs were dedicated to it. Donald was amused to discover vast amounts of resources were dedicated to some great race to get to it. The objective, as far as Donald could gather, was merely to stand on it, take a few pictures and come back.

It was difficult to believe, even if you knew otherwise, that the blanket of stars above the Moon held billions of other worlds, races and faces. He reminded himself how lucky he was to have seen this perspective of the universe. Merely looking up at the stars caused his heart to swell in his chest and he rejoiced inwardly as pure calm reigned supreme in his body. Suddenly, a dog barked and scared the crap out of him. Damn this place, he thought.

As he lolloped on, his great long, spindly legs stretching ahead of his body, he resolved to go back and see Polly tomorrow and talk to her properly about why he was here.

Perhaps this might be a good time to pause our story. Grab a cup of tea and settle down, as we get to know Donald a little more through the medium of the *Mentor Tome*.

What better place to start than with the most useless piece of information, his age. Donald was 84 in Overthere revolutions, 42 in Earth years. To confuse matters further, his appearance was that of a young man in his late 30s.

For those of you not previously acquainted with the *Mentor Tome* it acted as a sort of Overian guide to becoming an envoy on Earth.

Mentor Tome: Earth Edition
Requirement 1

All envoy applicants must be over the age of 50 revolutions. *

Approximately two revolutions per one Earth-year. Earth-years measured as per the Gregorian calendar.

Mentor Tome: Earth Edition
Requirement 2

All envoy applicants must appear more youthful than they are.

Post the Great Cosmic Revolt, these age and youth requirements had, over time, lost some of their original importance. They were now seen as ageist.

Mentor Tome: Earth Edition
Requirement 3

Not everything in the Mentor Tome should be taken literally. * Try to have a sense of proportion and context when reading it.

In case this is unclear, the applicant is urged to consider this: if a unicorn is a figment of the imagination, yet only distinguishable from a horse by its horn, then how can we spot them?

Thankfully, the authors had the foresight to include 'Requirement 3', which conveniently got around the problems in 'Requirement 2', although the unicorn theory was really confusing and almost unnecessary.

'Requirement 1', however, was vital. The *Mentor Tome* states it is crucial to be at least 50 revolutions. Any younger and the envoy could not physically cope with the pressure from the level of gravity surrounding the Earth's atmosphere. Overthere's low gravity environment meant they never had to deal with problems such as deterioration of muscle and bone density or anxiety and panic attacks.

Mentor Tome: Earth Edition
Requirement 4

When adopting an Earth character, deciding a profession will be of utmost importance, especially in western countries.*

Accountancy or low-level finance administration is ideal. Other options include estate agents, advertising, recruitment, tax collectors and traffic wardens.

*The second most asked human to human question is 'What do you do?' based on data collected in the USA and Europe, see requirements 147 for specific regional variances.

The primary objective of your Earth character was to blend in and remain indistinguishable. The data concluded that these professions were the least likely to attract interest. The result was that no one would talk to you at parties and, in the improbable event that you were invited, it was generally acceptable to have very few friends.

Back in the park, in the middle of a mini meltdown over the dog barking, Donald wrestled with his complex mind as he picked up his pace. He hurried along poky, dark streets littered with newspapers, signposts and potholes, while mentally listing the things he had to do in work the next day. There was a 10:30 am meeting that filled him with dread. The worst thing, by far, Donald had encountered on Earth and the thing he disliked more than dogs, panic attacks and people banging on about the Moon, was having to be an accountant.

Sadly, it was out of his hands somewhat, as it was a direct requirement from the *Mentor Tome* and Donald was a 'by the book' type. He liked process and order.

The 10:30 am weekly meeting with his boss was Donald's least favourite and, he was a significant factor for inducing the side effects of level four gravity panic. Gary Pootlepool was notoriously difficult to please. In the two years that Donald had worked for him, he felt it was Gary Pootlepool's sole mission to make his life an utter misery.

Donald suspected the main problem was that he was exceptionally talented with numbers, which made him a terrible accountant. He accurately recorded and genuinely balanced the accounts, exposing every backhander and overinflated growth projection. Still, only another four years and Donald would be free to choose a career of his liking according to the *Mentor Tome*. Four years was the probation period on Earth and, once completed, meant he would be fully integrated.

He promised himself he'd do something worthwhile, like become a nurse or join a charity. Donald was now beginning to understand why all these humans scurried around like worker ants in a semi-religious fashion day after day. It was a far more comfortable life than having to think about anything meaningful.

Eventually, he found himself in froFnt of the tube station. As he boarded the eastbound train back to Earls Court, he reflected on his previous encounter with Polly. It could have gone a lot better. Replaying their conversation in his head, he allowed his thoughts to wander.

Something was pleasing about her, but what it was he couldn't quite put his finger on. Attractions and attachments were primitive on Overthere, so this wasn't something Donald considered. But she smelt good and reminded him of something a bit like home. One thing he could not work out was why she was so fascinated by the paper the code was written on. What was that about? he pondered. He'd not expected those question at all. Still, he was pleased she hadn't asked who he was or where Bert was. He wasn't confident with his previously rehearsed answers and was glad he didn't have to use them.

A stream of conscious worry rattled through his head. He resolved to go and see her straight after work tomorrow and try to be of more help. Perhaps she could even be his friend. He missed having friends. He'd only known two friends during his Earth life, and he hadn't seen either of them for quite some time. Donald wrapped up in his thoughts, failed to recognise the pattern of activity around him and paid no attention to the well-dressed women sat opposite him in the carriage.

All the connected signs were there, but he'd overlooked them. Had he paid more attention to the woman sat opposite him and the strategically placed suits positioned by the carriage doors, then perhaps he would have changed lines before Earls Court. Maybe he would have made his 10:30 am meeting with Gary Pootlepool and honoured his post-work visit to Polly. Indeed, he wouldn't have chosen this precise moment to have a little nap.

As his mind started to drift, he became lulled by the soft rattle of a thousand glass bottles bumping into one another, as the old carriages juddered along. His thoughts toppled over one another and started to expand out of shape. Quietly, and without knowing it, he had slipped into another world. The slow shudder of the train increased into a gallop of what could only be described as stampeding horse-elephants. He felt a bit sick and couldn't quite work out what he was supposed to be doing. Ahead of him was, what looked like, a village with tiny huts. There was no way of stopping the stampede, so he just held on to what he thought was the reins, dug in his heels and prepared himself to trample all over the little village huts. As he got closer and closer, he was suddenly wrenched back into reality and jolted awake.

His eyes seemed to be covered. He was no longer on the tube train, but outside somewhere. With his cuffed his hands behind his back, he felt two people either side dragging him along. He was violently sick, as a mixture of dizziness and fear collided together. No one around him said anything. They just kept pulling him towards an unknown space. He became aware of more people around him, not only two at the side. In the distance he could hear the screeching sound of trains and the pulse of traffic. He couldn't have been asleep for long, but his nose felt sore. He sniffed a couple of times and detected an unidentified chemical smell.

Donald's instinct told him not to ask any questions. His best bet now was to pretend he'd blacked out. He let his body go limp again and felt the hands either side grip tighter to hoist him along. Donald didn't need to ask any questions anyway, as questions were pointless. This ambush was inevitable, and he'd trained for it.

What he needed was time to prepare himself. He needed to be mindful and watchful. Fortunately, Donald understood that time was relative to the individual. He carefully moved his mind into kidnap mode. It was all part of his envoy training and he knew it well. The reality was far more terrifying than the theory. He recalled the *Mentor Tome*, skipping directly to the relevant part. Donald skilfully slowed down his breathing, running through the following mantra:

> One, we are one, we are alone, we are all one.
> Become everything, become nothing.

He repeated this the required number of times and felt familiar waves of calm envelop him. Now he had achieved calmness, he needed to identify and lock away his mind's secrets and throw away the key.

Absorbed in this mental task, another part of his mind practised watchfulness. He became the observer of his own body. Being blindfolded was useful, as it heightened his other senses.

He detected five people around him – two in front, two either side and one behind. It must be dark, as every couple of steps, one of the two men either side of him would stumble as if they couldn't quite see where they were going. The ones holding him were male, perhaps late 20s or early 30s. The slightly stubbly hair on the back of their hands against his, firm skin and the faint whiff of body odour, gave him the confirmation he needed. He also detected two females, with a different smell. Their heavy dairy diet scent made him gag slightly.

Reaching their destination, Donald could no longer feel the night breeze. Freshly moulded plastic that lingered in newer cars and leather replaced the outside air. Having run through the required protocol, with all his secrets safely locked away, he now focused on his final step. With all the strength he could muster to blot out his surroundings, he slipped into a dream-filled sleep.

His captors would meet him soon enough.

Chapter 4. Introducing Bert

'We are sorry to announce the 14:45 from Bristol Parkway to London Paddington is delayed by approximately eight minutes and will arrive on time at 14:45 on platform four,' announced the monotone voice. Well now, Bert thought to himself, who could have guessed that Great Rails would be the first invent commercial time travel, as he adjusted his watch for the second time.

An icy wind whipped its way along the platform, causing a ripple of coat hugging and grumbles. Bert pulled up the collar on his paper-thin linen shirt and silently cursed Great Rails for the umpteenth time. Rechecking his watch, he noticed that his hands looked old and shrivelled. For the first time in ages, Bert felt old and kicked out at a passing pigeon in annoyance. Too old, too fat, too stupid, Bert knew he shouldn't think about it too much, for the sake of his sanity. This country is the pits, he silently fumed. To distract himself he gazed into the distance, resting his attention on a sizeable dilapidated warehouse.

When Bert was a small boy, he would imagine what it might be like to work in a warehouse. He was never too sure what it was that people did in warehouses, other than wander around a bit with hard hats on, but he'd had a feeling that it would be exciting and vital. He'd taken to making himself a hard hat from a washing up bowl that his parents had. Bert adored the idea of working in a warehouse. In his childhood play, he'd set himself a to-do list for the day and carry out all his tasks assiduously, pacing up and down a lot, pointing at things and navigating the parking of imaginary forklift trucks.

'The 14:45 is further delayed by approximately 18 minutes, it will be arriving on platform four at 14:45.' Bert was momentarily roused from his thoughts by this update and adjusted his watch accordingly.

Polly would be so pleased to see him. She might be a bit funny at first, but he'd left her the house and money, what more could she want? Why did she always want so much from him? Janet Planet came into his mind, with her beautiful young face and long silver-blonde hair. She was flawless, and those bastards had killed her. Catching a glimpse of an approaching train, he was momentarily roused out of his mausoleum mind.

Safely nestled in his train compartment, Bert settled into the steady humming sounds of high-speed rails at work. Involuntary feelings of despair started to creep into his bones, like a dirty paintbrush dipping into his mind until the whole clear pot of water turned a muddy grey. His heart seemed gripped by the bones in his chest.

Polly had been only 16 when he'd left home. He wondered whether she'd changed much in the last 11 years. Despite telling himself he'd done the right thing, Bert suffered greatly in coming to terms with his choices. It was as if he were two different men with two conflicting agendas. Bert was ashamed of the man he was, and the one he failed to be. And yet, he still deserved a life, didn't he?

He comforted himself in knowing Polly would be OK. By taking over guardianship of his younger sister in these tragic circumstances, he had done his best. Transferring their beautiful, cosy flat in Putney into her name; she'd certainly been okay with that. It was evident to him that she relished the idea of him going but was trying to hide it rather badly. Polly had done lots of skipping around, loudly shouting 'Freedom' when she thought he wasn't paying attention, yet it did little to convince Bert he had made the right decision by her.

She had a roof over her head, enough stationery to set up a small concern and a student loan that would supply her with enough alcohol for a few years without killing her. He'd even organised a weekly fruit and vegetable box to be delivered, to ensure Polly was reminded what a vegetable looked like. Yet, many other brothers would not have bothered as much as him.

He smiled when he recalled the last conversation they'd had in the Worm and Duck, sipping flat cider and sharing a bag of dry roasted peanuts.

> 'This is boring isn't it,' said Polly tactfully.

> 'You could pretend you're a bit sad,' replied Bert, bored to tears.

> 'Yeah, yeah I am…probably. But it's a bit exciting, isn't it? You're going travelling around the world for a year and now I'm an adult. It's a fresh start for both of us and it's only a year. It'll fly by.'

Bert had intended to only go for a year. Did he know he'd be gone for 10? Walking away from the pub that day, after giving Polly a brief, awkward hug, Bert had a feeling that returning after a year was unlikely. He returned to looking moody, and what he hoped was distinguished-looking, as the green fields blasted by the train window.

Chapter 5. Polly makes a plan

> We start, then, with nothing...
>
> Charles S. Peirce, *Logic of Events*, 1898.

Once back in her flat, Polly felt utterly exhausted suddenly, so set about making herself a nice cup of Lady Grey. Her apartment, with its beautifully tiled flooring, ancient rugs and high ceilings, was her pride, joy and sanctuary. In her kitchen, she had all the things to help with her baking – lots of jars with mysterious-looking stuff in them and several plants in various stages of health. Picking at a ginger cake she'd made earlier, she looked out of the large, arched window onto the common. It was too dark to make out anything, other than the outline of trees, but she wasn't looking at them.

She sat on the sofa and, no sooner had she leant back, she jumped back up again as she remembered the entire point of the visit – that bit of paper! She spent a crazed couple of minutes, which felt like an eternity, scouring around for it. She thought she'd lost it and was very nearly on the verge of breaking down and throwing herself on the floor in complete contempt of her ineptitude, when she spotted a scrap of paper innocently lying on the table in the hall. At first, she was so excited. Excitement quickly turned to bafflement as she attempted to work out what this piece of paper was trying to tell her. It simply said:

www.nothing.com

Heaving her laptop onto her lap and firing up the interwebs, she considered for the trillionth time investing in a new one. It made a sort of whirring noise then promptly died. Damn, damn, damn! She got up and dumped the whole heap of junk in the bin. Locating her phone, she was momentarily distracted by a message from Tobi asking how she was. Did she like him? She still hadn't responded to his previous messages, so she guessed not. He was attentive, polite and emotionally available. She wanted to like him but...

Her phone battery dropped from 87% to 2% and also promptly died; she'd left her charger at work. Polly could hear her mother's voice in her head telling her off for daydreaming about silly little boys instead of focusing. Clutching at her head, Polly wandered into the kitchen to search for something comforting. The clock showed it was 12:45 am. How on earth had that happened?

There was nothing for it but to wait until morning. If Polly went to bed now, she could then get up at 5 am and be in the office for 6 am. She shuddered, 5 am was surely the middle of the night. Still, the burning desire to know or understand what on earth had happened tonight was enough for her. Polly ruefully resigned herself to bed. After much faffing around and another cup of tea, she switched on her digital radio and climbed into bed. She lay there in the dark, half-listening to the melodic sound of Shostakovich's second movement. Her eyes wide open and mind running round and round, trying to resolve the unusual events of the evening. There was no resolution for tonight, and by the looks of things, no chance of sleep either.

Light harassed her eyes as they adjusted from pleasant dark slumber to dawn. Outside wasn't particularly sunny; closer inspection revealed a blanket of endless off-white cloud. Polly had developed a method over the years to distract from her unpleasant thoughts and places. She would select a few things she liked and focus on them, ignoring everything else.

Every workday morning, Polly faced two options when she left her house. She could turn left out of her house, skip alongside the park, around the beautiful lake, glance at the curious house with the high iron gates and head down to the overland train, which was the far less ugly route to work. Alternatively, she could turn right and walk up the painstaking hill, past the run-down garage with the strange and nonsensical 'Madagascar' neon sign, up onto the high street with the endless fried chicken 'restaurants' and cram herself onto the bus, with its steamed-up windows and anxious commuters. It was a tricky choice. Although not all that tricky, because every day Polly turns right to save herself time. Polly was eternally late, and today was no exception. Time is always the cruel dictator that gets in the way of dreams, or perhaps it is other people's dependence on time that's the problem.

There was one particular tree she passed that she was fond of. In summer, this mighty chestnut boasted thousands of luscious, green leaves and spiky balls that would turn golden brown in late autumn, pleasingly littering the entire street with foliage and a scattering of shiny, deep brown conkers. The tree was directly opposite the garage with the weird neon sign and yet she instinctively didn't like it. She didn't know why, perhaps it was because it looked so hopeless and grotty, so she ignored it. Beyond the tree was a small patch of grass with a handful of pretty, pink flowers that would spring up in the early part of the year. She used to think they were delphiniums, until she looked this up. The next spot was the old town hall, which was a combination of majestic, Edwardian red-brick and mischievous, creeping ivy. It was this that thrilled her eye, as she imagined all sorts of exciting things happening in the building over the last hundred-odd years.

When she had finally drifted off to sleep, sometime after 3 am, she'd had a particularly disturbing dream. She couldn't remember the details, neither could she shake off the feeling. Vague hints of a mundane background and grubby room sloshed their way around her mind. Some form of turbulence was taking place, which she had no control over. Equally, there was a sense of responsibility for something. But what?

Her memory of the dream began to settle. The real-world memories began to take shape and started to join again like little ice crystals on a pane of glass. Donald's visit, the piece of paper, the strange late evening interruption. What had she been thinking pre-10:25 pm? She had no clue nor care now. Whatever it was, she replayed everything over and over in her mind. Had she missed something?

Passing the town hall, she reached the crossing at the busy main road. With one arm, she expertly scrambled around in her shoulder bag for the piece of paper. Her hand closed around it and, as she waited for the little man in the box to flash green, she wrenched the piece of paper from her bag to ogle it for the hundredth time. In a purple ink pen in the centre of the irrelevant A4 paper was written:

    www.nothing.com

What on earth could it mean? She ran to catch the overcrowded bus and wished, for the first time, the journey to work would go quickly.

It wasn't as if Polly hated going to work. She liked most of the people and was well-regarded, albeit unknown, most of the time. The work wasn't a problem. She enjoyed managing a project and measuring its progress to completion. The main problem for her was the overwhelming pointlessness of the work and the pretence that the company was somehow saving the universe by selling ringtones. Everyone in her office seemed to be divided between two camps. Those unaware of the pointlessness of their existence, who kept quiet, and the ones who knew it was pointless but enjoyed making others as unhappy as possible, without committing physical violence.

As she entered the office, she no longer cared. Something had changed. She had felt the shift within her overnight; for once she had a real-life challenge on her hands. And it was bloody exciting. She felt bigger things were at play. At least she did, that was, until she spent the first hour of the day in a meeting with the senior management team, which consisted of 19 people, accounting for 19% of the workforce and 81% of the wages. The conference itself was the 'Bi-daily London Short Term Update Summit', which was in some inconceivable way different to the 'Weekly London Mid-Term Update Summit' and the 'Bi-weekly London Long-Term Update Summit'.

Arriving on the dot of 9 am, Polly had no time before the meeting to get near her desk. The hour passed painfully slow, when at last, at 10:05 am, she escaped. The encounter left Polly as it usually did, with a sense that all the colour had drained out of the world until she remembered her quest. Polly was dying to tell someone what had happened last night but knew the scepticism it would be met with. She wanted to keep it to herself, to protect this little flame of hope so she could evaluate things properly, without others' intrusions.

Once back at her computer, she typed in *www.nothing.com*. She was careful to type it out accurately, despite her bubbling excitement. The page that loaded had no navigable links and a cheap-looking logo for something called Nothing Ventures Inc. Underneath there was one sentence that read:

>We start, then, with nothing...

Polly refreshed the page a couple of times, but the same inconclusive message was there. She sat looking blankly at the screen as her mind whizzed through all the possibilities. Maybe it was some sort of code, like a cryptic crossword. Polly had never been very good at those. She quickly checked her calendar. Thankfully, she had no meetings for the rest of the morning, which gave her time to think. A million thought avenues had opened in her mind. The sheer number made her mind lock. She suddenly remembered a piece of advice a good friend of hers once gave her. His tactic, when faced with a problem, would be to spend as many hours as possible researching all the information at hand, then have a bottle of wine, a good meal and sleep on it. The next morning, he would swear the path ahead would reveal itself. Did Polly have the patience for waiting another 24 hours? No. Forget it.

She opened a new Google document and created a file named 'Project Plan 1.0'. A title innocuous enough that no one would bother to read it. In the first tab, she noted down what she had to go on.

Polly typed in the quote 'We start, then, with nothing...' into her browser and found it to be a quote by Charles Sanders Peirce. The full passage read:

> We start, then, with nothing, pure zero. But this is not the nothing of negation. For not means other than, and other is merely a synonym of the ordinal numeral second. As such it implies a first; while the present pure zero is prior to every first. The nothing of negation is the nothing of death, which comes second to, or after, everything. But this pure zero is the nothing of not having been born. There is no individual thing, no compulsion, outward nor inward, no law. It is the germinal nothing, in which the whole universe is involved or foreshadowed. As such, it is absolutely undefined and unlimited possibility – boundless possibility.

> There is no compulsion and no law. It is boundless freedom.

It didn't make a great deal of sense to Polly, who was not renowned for her deep philosophical understanding. She couldn't even spell philosophical. It certainly didn't tell her the key to everything, nor bring her whatever it was she desired, nor infinite amounts of power. It did, however, give her an idea. There were only two ways to get to the bottom of this.

Polly wrote down two actions:

1. Find Donald
2. Find Bert Fairwold

Something else had occurred to her as she remembered what Donald had told her about the code. If she recalled correctly, he had said that the code would bring her whatever she desired. Well, thought Polly, what is it that I want?

She added a third action to the list, possibly the most challenging task yet, not that the first two were a walk in the park:

3. Find out what I want

Polly dedicated her brain to the first action. Only knowing Donald's first name, she could only think to ask – how many people in the world are called Donald? The answer to this question turned out to be a lot. Most of them living in the US, where 99.87% were male. Polly took a moment to feel sorry for the 0.13% of females named Donald. After several other fruitless searches, she decided to type in 'Donald and Charles Sanders Peirce'. Hurrah! Polly wiggled with excitement in her chair as her eye was drawn to the second link on the page.

> ### 28th September, Economics section, Accountancy, *Globalisation to Universalisation* by Donald Pigeon.
> How could universalisation ever possibly work? Many say it would be impossible and too big for our brains to handle. But, then I refer you to Charles Sanders Peirce 'At first, we start...'

She clicked on the link and briefly skimmed through the article. It might have been written in another language, but she wasn't interested in the content. It just had to be Donald, she thought. It was too much of a coincidence. She scrolled down to the bottom of the page. There was no photograph, but now she had his full name and what he did, which was accountancy. It was weird, he did not look that boring. The rest was easy peasy, she quickly located the firm where, according to *Int-r-linked*, he was currently working and managed to find the address.

If she jumped in a cab it would take her less than 10 minutes to get there. But what about work? Sod it, she could pop out now. Getting to the bottom of this felt more important than lunch, yet she sat for a moment in a state of indecision. Would she get told off? she wondered. It seemed ridiculous that an adult would be worried about this. Unknowingly, and almost unthinkingly, she took out her phone, opened the little yellow taxi app and hit 'Pick me up here'. Her phone flashed instantly: 'Your cab is 1 minute away'. That settled it. She picked up her bag and ran out of the building into the waiting taxi.

'Where to love?' The cab driver eyed her through the mirror.

Polly read out the address she had jotted down and the cab driver frowned.

'OK, no problem. There's a bit of traffic on the Strand this morning, but I can just cut up through Covent Garden, if that's ok with you?'

Polly, having lived in London for 15 years, had no idea if this was better or not, but put on the show of goodwill required.

'So, what do you do then love?' asked the cabbie making a death-defying U-turn.

'Me?' As if there was someone else that he might have been talking to. 'Oh well, I don't do anything that interesting to be honest.' Polly wondered how to aggrandise project management.

'You got a meeting then?'

'No I don't.' Polly realised she was desperate to tell someone the events of the last 24 hours to the point of bursting and, given the anonymity of the back seat of a cab, she felt free to unburden herself. 'It's a bit of a bizarre story actually.'

'Oh yeah? What's been going on then?' She caught his eye in the mirror to see she had piqued his interest.

'Well, it's all going to sound a bit strange.' She continued

'I've been driving a cab around London for 40 years love, nothing surprises me anymore.'

'Well, it started last night. Unexpectedly, this bloke turned up at my house, about 10:45 pm'

'That's a bit late to turn up unannounced.' The cabbie frowned a her in the mirror.

'I know, that's what I thought. Anyway, he said his name was Donald and' Polly reeled off the whole story, missing nothing, even explaining briefly about her prediction of her brother's apparent involvement.

'The weird thing is, I haven't even seen Bert, that's my brother, for nearly 10 years but I'm pretty sure this Donald knows him.' Polly picked at a bit of fluff on the seat.

'Always trust your instincts, they very rarely served me wrong in life. Have you got the piece of paper with the code on it?' He was fully involved in the mystery now.

'Yeah, look. It's just a bit of paper.' She leaned forward and handed the driver the folded paper she'd been carrying around.

The driver looked it over, nodded knowingly and handed it back.

'And you reckon this bloke Donald is one of them then, from Overthere I mean?' The cabbie couldn't quite bring himself to say the 'A' word, for fear of discrediting the story.

'Well, I think so. I don't know how to tell though. I felt he was different somehow. I could be wrong.'

'Nah I think you're spot on love. I've had the same thing myself a few times,' he said, not to be outdone on the new story stakes. 'I was saying to my wife, June, just last night, I said I reckon I've been driving around loads of ali...' He stopped himself just in time. 'People from Overthere. I know what you mean about that sort of feeling, they don't look any different to us, do they? But you just know.'

Oh, great, thought Polly, he's a nutter (then reminded herself of her circumstances before she threw any more stones and brought down her frail glasshouse). They sat in comfortable silence for a few moments, both reviewing what the other had said.

'So, what about this code then? Do you think it's legit?' he piped up again.

'I don't know, and I don't know how to work it out.' Polly again scratched her head.

'Have you tried it?' he asked keenly.

'What do you mean?' asked Polly, genuinely confused.

'Well, suppose it's like the genie in the lamp. Didn't this Daniel bloke...'

'Donald. His name is Donald,' interrupted Polly, as it mattered.

'Ah yeah sorry. Didn't Donald say you could do whatever you want and it gave you loads of power or something? The answer to everything.'

'Yes, well, that's what he said,' Polly nodded.

'Well, have you tried it like a lamp? Have you rubbed the bit of paper and wished for anything?' The jokey laugh at the end of this statement told Polly he was semi-serious.

Polly snorted with laughter. 'No, I haven't. Do you think I should? I didn't even know what to wish for.'

'Yeah go on, try it. Let's see if it's that. You'll feel like an idiot if you didn't try. For a start, you can wish that this traffic would clear.'

'Alright then. Let's hope a bloody big genie doesn't turn up, otherwise we might crash.'

'Not in this traffic love,' he nodded out at the backed-up cars littering the road.

Polly held the piece of paper in her hand. Feeling ridiculous, she rubbed the writing on the paper and said out-loud, 'I wish this traffic would clear.'

Both Polly and the driver looked about them, not sure what to expect. After a minute, they had accepted nothing was likely to happen and both felt foolish.

The cabbie spoke first. 'You know what I reckon love? I reckon your brother is pulling your leg, and he's, hang on...' He cut his evaluation short as, mysteriously, the traffic in front started to move. 'Well, would you look at that!' They caught each other's eye in the mirror, both clearly excited but still in disbelief. 'Hey, you should wish for a billion pounds now,' the cabbie said, only half-joking.

'What if you're right about it working like a genie? Then I only get three wishes and I've just used one up clearing the traffic,' said Polly, and she was only two-thirds joking.

'Yeah, fair point. Then I suppose you should have a proper good think about what you want then. Oh, here we are. This is the building you want.' Polly could tell he was disappointed for their journey to end, as was she. 'I tell you what love – oh I'm Tony, by the way – I was going to go on me break any way. I'll hang around here for the next half hour and you can tell me what happens when you come out, then I'll drop you back for free. That a deal?'

'Deal.' Polly beamed at him. What a nice guy, she thought. 'Cheers Tony,' she shouted jumping out the cab and turning back give him a double thumbs-up.

'Good luck love.' Tony waved back, turned into a side street, parked up and awaited her return.

AccountingIT was your standard, glass-fronted power office, with all the soul removed. Inside, the reception boasted exposed pipes and silver air conditioning shafts, that looked to Polly a bit like a Blue Peter replica of a space station gone wrong; she hoped all the pipes were massive cardboard loo rolls wrapped in tin foil.

The man sitting behind reception looked bored and uncomfortable in his shiny, blue security uniform. Now this was happening, Polly felt nervous. In her mind she switched to the mode that she always adopted in meetings; just look confident and bored, she told herself.

'Hi there, good morning, I'm here to see Donald Pigeon.'

The security guard barely looked up as he passed her a clipboard with columns like a petition on it.

'Can you fill this in? What's your name? Do you have an appointment?' He spoke in a stern voice, as if he ran the place and her being there was an inconvenience to his otherwise jam-packed schedule of welcoming people to the building.

Polly considered giving a false name for a second, then thought the better of it. She had trouble enough remembering her details, let alone fictitious ones.

'My name is Polly Fairwold, and yes he is expecting me for our 11 am.' Alright, easy James Bond, no need for additional details, keep it simple. She glanced at the clock and was relieved to find it's 10:55 am.

'I'll call him down now. Please take a seat.' The man weakly indicated behind her.

'Thank you,' says Polly, and in her head added, and such a pleasure to meet you too.

Walking over to the so-called seating area, surrounded with chairs that any human being would find impossible to sit on without looking like a total dick, Polly opted for the least painful looking one, a triangle-shaped, green felt covered boulder.

Seeing the security guard put down the phone, she assumed Donald was on his way. What am I going to say to him? Or worse still, what if it isn't him at all? Polly had prepared nothing for their encounter. She got out her notepad and pen to list possible questions:

1. How do you know Bert?
2. Where is Bert?
3. What is this code? How do I work it out?
4. Are you from another planet?
5.

She leaves number 5 blank, in case something else springs to mind in the next few minutes, but can't think what else she needs to know. She hopes that if they get to the bottom of those first 3, then she could improvise from there.

Her thoughts are interrupted by a man in a blue, checked shirt and chinos standing in front of her.

'Polly Fairwold?' he asks.

Damn, this is the wrong Donald after all. Now what? Polly jumped up.

'My name is Gary Pootlepool. Donald works for me.' He seemed very pleased with himself as he announced this.

'Yes, I am Polly, nice to meet you,' offering a hand to shake. Ok, Polly thinks, I'm just going to have to wing this.

'Yes, unfortunately, Donald has not turned up to work today. I checked his diary, and I couldn't find your meeting. I'm not sure what the nature of your meeting is. Donald has neglected to leave any proper handover notes in place of his absence.'

Donald has not turned up for work today. That didn't sound to Polly as if Gary Pootlepool knew where Donald was. She thought on her feet and said quickly, 'Yes I know, that's why I'm here. I'm a... friend...of Donald's and have been trying to get hold of him. We were supposed to be having dinner last night, but he didn't turn up, so I thought I'd come and check on him today.' Polly smiled sweetly at him.

'Oh.' Gary's tone quickly went from helpful to passive aggressive. 'Donald missed a crucial meeting this morning. It's very unprofessional, and we're very concerned.'

'Have you tried his mobile number? Do you have the same one as I have?' Polly said, taking her phone out of her pocket. Desperately trying to remember how many digits a mobile number was supposed to have, she read out a made-up number.

Gary Pootlepool, not to appear rude, took out his phone and read out the number he had stored for Donald. Polly typed it into her phone.

'If you happen to reach him can you tell him to contact me immediately,' Gary grunted, reminding Polly of her boss.

She was, however, grateful for his lack of concern. Someone more compassionate might have tried to contact the police to report a missing person. That would have led to all sorts of difficult questions.

'Thank you for your help Gary. I will let him know as soon as I've got hold of him,' she said, trying to sound like a worried friend.

Gary Pootlepool, pleased she wasn't going to hang around bothering him any longer, graciously added as an afterthought, 'You should try his house.'

'Good idea, thank you, I will,' said Polly, shaking his hand and backing out of the building. She turned and walked quickly towards the door, grateful to get out of this miserable hellhole.

'Madam excuse me!' the security guard shouted at her from behind the desk, making everyone turn to look at Polly, the culprit.

Oh crap, thought Polly, what now?

'Can you sign out,' he said, as if she'd just broken the law.

Relieved, Polly dashed back and scribbled in the last column on the clipboard, turned and marched out into the fresh air and busy mid-morning London street.

Polly spotted Tony's cab just off to the side of the building. Unfortunately, it was empty. Polly walked over anyway and saw Tony coming out of the coffee shop across the road. He looked up and, seeing Polly, waved. Polly waved back.

'Well that was quick,' he said, 'I've only had time to pick up a tea and the paper. What happened?'

She took the tea he handed her, so he could climb back into the driver seat, then handed it back.

'He didn't turn up for work today,' explained Polly, wondering if she should get back in the cab and if the update warranted the previously promised free ride.

'Oh damn,' said Tony, genuinely understanding how annoying this development was. 'Jump in and I can drop you back. We'll have a think together.'

'Brilliant, thank you. Again, this is kind of you.' Pleased that he'd said 'we', she felt this needed double brain power.

'Not at all love. I can't keep calling you love all day. What's your name?'

'It's Polly.'

'As in "put the kettle on"?'

Polly laughed at this. Tony was not the first to point this out, and by no means would be the last, but she genuinely didn't mind at all; it felt comfortable and used to be a fun family joke, stretching the meaning of the word 'fun', as all families did.

'So, where now then Aladdin?' Tony asked, reminding her of their earlier conversation.

'I supposed back to work,' said Polly.

'Really? Seems like a waste of the day. I bet Aladdin didn't have to go back to work,' Tony joked with her.

'Could I wish I didn't have to go back to work?' said Polly, seriously considering it.

'No need to waste a wish for that love, that's within your power. Let me tell you something – 20 years ago I had a job in the city, a lot of money it was, even back then. One day, I get this big promotion for selling a load of shares in Oil or something. I can't remember anyway. So I get this big pay rise and promotion, and I know I'm supposed to be happy and think about all that money, but inside I don't feel anything but cold. Back then, June and I had only just married. We'd never had a lot of money, see. I thought, now we are loaded everything would be easy, and I'd be happy. When I get home that night, I tell her. She looks me straight in the eye and says, "Tell me you're happy." I said, "I'm happy." She said, "You're a bad liar Tony." That was it. I went back the next day and handed in my notice. I felt like I'd won the lottery.' He leaned back in his seat.

'Wow I bet that was amazing. I bet you had to get another job quickly. What about your house?' Polly asked.

'Well, here's the funny thing. A mate of mine from school was a cabbie and he asked if I could cover for him for a few days. I had nothing better to do, so I said "sure", and that was it. I never looked back. Many people choose being in the City for the status and the money, but to real people none of that matters,' he chuckled to himself.

'Do you think life would be different if you'd stayed and made a load of money in the City?' Polly searched his big, soft, grey-brown eyes for any sniff of fibs.

'Who says I haven't?' he chipped in with a wink. 'I've been the boss for 20 years. I pick up all the best information in here and I can work and think on other things. No one pays you any attention when you're the driver, but even if I hadn't done well financially,' a touch of purple touched his bristly cheeks, 'it wouldn't have made much of a difference. We don't need much to live a good life. Love, food, warmth, a good bed and good company. The rest of it, that's made up to make us buy more things.' He went on stroking his chin as if he was on a shaving advert. 'I guess I was lucky to have June. I feel sorry for those wealthy ones. You have to wonder what they are up against in here,' he tapped the side of his head. 'Something terrible has happened to them, I reckon, to keep needing that much.' Polly thought he might cry, so hastily looked away.

Polly rarely wondered what she's missed out on by not having her parents around, but for a moment was painfully reminded. Somehow, she'd forgotten what it was like to breathe; she'd forgotten that she was free, that no one was making her go to work.

'Good point,' said Polly out loud. Before thinking about it too much, she whipped her phone out of her pocket and sent a text to her boss, feigning a family emergency, which was sort of half right.

'Done!' she exclaimed.

'Cor blimey Polly, me and my mouth! Right, so where now? Don't worry about how far it is, I'm taking an early lunch too, you've inspired me.' Tony looked at her with a hint of pride.

'I haven't a clue. Perhaps it's a good idea if I head home. Is it too early to want to go to the pub?' Polly wondered out loud.

'I tell you what, you tell me where home is, and we'll head back. I'll drop you at your local pub and you can get me a drink as payment.' Tony took a small rag out of his pocket and polished the rear-view mirror.

'An excellent plan. It's Putney, so you might regret that,' she said, giving him the chance to back out.

'Used to live around there myself. To Putney! Now, what happened in there? How did you find out he hadn't turned up?' Tony asked, as he threw them out into the manic London traffic.

The journey was a lot quicker than Polly imagined it would be to get out west. She was half expecting to spend the next week stuck in the back of the cab, but what felt like a few minutes later, they found themselves in the Worm and Duck public house with their drinks in hand. The barman gave her a look that said, 'What are you doing here this early?' But then quickly lost interest and got back to his crossword, leaving them both in peace in the empty pub.

'So,' began Tony supping at his half of real ale, amusingly named 'Badgers Arse'. 'He's still not answering then?' he asked, as Polly put her phone down on the table.

'It's not ringing anymore, it's just a dead tone. That's odd isn't it, that it's now dead? Going to answerphone I could understand, but the dead tone suggests it's cut off.'

'I don't know about these things love,' said Tony thoughtfully.

Polly took a long glug of her cider and rubbed her head, as if trying to warm up her brain and stimulate it into action.

'I've been thinking about what you said earlier about what it is I want, and I've been thinking about that quote, the Charles S. Peirce one. There's something in that.' Polly scrunched up her face almost as she could push her brain to pop out the answer.

Tony let her think on some more.

'Before yesterday, I hadn't ever thought about what I wanted. I was just doing the things in front of me. Then I get given this code and now I'm here, even though I had nothing to go on.' Polly felt a bubble of excitement, like she'd stepped out into wide-open space.

Tony laughed.

'What is it?' she asked.

'Well that's it, isn't it! You literally had nothing to go on,' he nodded at the piece of paper in with 'www.nothing.com' inscribed. 'But from that nothing, now you're here, and you've met me, less than 24 hours later.'

'Well I haven't got very far, have I?' said Polly, dismayed.

'Haven't you?' continued Tony. 'It seems to me that yesterday you had nothing, and today you have a mission. You need to find your brother, you need to find Donald and you need to know what you want more than anything. Plus, you've made friends with a top bloke called Tony.' He winked at her during this last bit.

'You're right! I hadn't thought about it, but yes, things have changed already,' Polly brightened.

'I think your brother has got something to do with this. I don't know how you'll find him, but you will. It might not seem as exciting if it's just your brother playing a prank. Perhaps you haven't got the code to power and whatnot, but today has been unpredictable and exciting, and that's a start.' Tony put down his glass and swiped his chin on his cuff.

Polly realised they'd both finished their drinks and was about to offer Tony another, when he said.

'Right I need to get back on the road. It's been a pleasure to meet you Polly. If you ever need anything here is my number.' He dug a slightly dogeared business card out of his wallet and handed it to her. 'Can I drop you off at your house?'

'Thank you Tony, and no, it's no problem, I can walk from here. I could do with the air.'

They got up and left the pub, shook hands and parted company.

Unpredictable and exciting, pondered Polly, now when was the last time her life had been like that?

Chapter 6. Tony and the doctor

Tony climbed back into his cab and watched Polly part run, part skip down the road and disappear out of sight. He let out an involuntary chuckle, what a morning. Tony wondered if he'd meet Polly again, he probably would. He was a cabbie; he could often see more than most, it was on account of the spare thinking time he got. Yes, I'll see that one again, no doubt about it.

Tiny pins of rain appeared on his windscreen. The sound was music to his ears. Nothing got bums on taxi seats like a bit of rain. He'd had enough fun for one morning. Mentally shaking himself, he switched on his phone. Almost immediately, it pinged through the next job just over Putney Bridge in Fulham. He paused briefly to clean his glasses and got on his way.

Tony arrived outside the Hurlingham Club. He'd not picked anyone up from here for years and had almost forgotten to take the Napier Avenue approach, due to the restricted access under Putney bridge station. Still, he'd made good time. The rain had now reached the heavy drizzle stage and was threatening a full storm. Tony peered out through his steamed-up window to spot his passenger. A very smartly dressed woman, Tony guessed in her early 50s, appeared outside and put up a large golfing umbrella.

He beeped his horn and flashed his lights, and she made her way to the cab. He wondered who she might be; the Hurlingham Club was not the most well-known private members' club, certainly not in Tony's circle of chums, but it was undoubtedly one of the most prestigious in the country. Whoever this lady was, she was well connected. Tony's interest was tickled. Today was an exciting day.

'Good Afternoon, can you take me to 49 Farringdon Road?' Her voice had an upper-class ring to it, coupled with an air of authority. Years of experience had taught Tony the difference between business and pleasure - this trip was most definitely the former.

'Certainly, jump on in,' Tony beamed at her.

They sat in silence for the first five minutes. Tony, naturally gifted at starting any conversation from scraps, asked, 'Have you had a good morning?'

The well-dressed woman looked up from her phone where she had been intently typing away. She caught his eye in the mirror of the taxi and looked back down at her phone. Manners were not high up on her, no doubt, vast skill set. She didn't even pretend to not hear him. Tony, however, was never one to be put off by a lack of response decided to continue anyway.

'I've had a funny one myself, really unusual actually.' He checked in the mirror again, this time she didn't even bother to look up. Good Tony thought, a bit of a challenge this one.

So, he went for something a little more provocative.

'Have you ever met an alien?' he asked, seemingly from nowhere.

The well-dressed women looked up sharply and met his eye again. Tony, who'd expected a reaction, was surprised at the effect his words had. He didn't know why this had grabbed her attention, but he'd play on this a little more.

'Why do you ask me that?' she said slowly, not once taking her eyes off him.

'It's just because of a curious incident that occurred to me and another passenger earlier today,' he said, careful not to give away too much.

She seemed to relax a little but not entirely as she asked, clearly despite herself, 'Why, what happened?'

It was the perfect opening. Tony launched headfirst into Polly's story. First explaining the code and then the small adventure of trying to find Donald. As he merrily chatted away, he became aware of how intently she was looking at him, almost a little incredulously, but more than that she was fascinated. He became a little more cautious about exact details; he wasn't sure what stopped him exactly. Still, his early warning system told him that, somehow, the very well-dressed lady was connected into his story and keener to hear it more than he found comfortable.

'...and so, that was my morning. Funny hey? How about you then? Had a busy one?' Tony quickly concluded.

The woman was clearly in no mood for small talk. 'The person that your passenger needed to find, did she say what his name was?' she asked.

'Um, no I don't think she said his name. Maybe she did. I can't remember now.' Tony tried to make a joke of it. 'The old mind wasn't what it was. My misses June, she says I'd forget my head if it wasn't screwed on and...'

He cut off mid-speech.

'Why did you ask me about aliens before and if I'd seen one? I thought you were going to tell me you'd met one yourself?' she asked. Again, something about her tone and the way she was looking at him made Tony careful to answer.

'Nah,' he laughed, 'I haven't seen one. It was just Polly and me, that was the passenger, we were joking around and thought that Donald might be an alien. He was the one who gave her the code. To be honest, I think it was just her brother having a laugh.' Nice one Tony, inwardly, kicking himself. He was not sure what he'd just given away, but he felt it was something pretty important.

The well-dressed woman leaned back in her seat, looking as if she'd got what she needed from the conversation. Tony felt a bit nervous; he rarely spoke about other passengers in detail, but he'd been so excited and inspired by the morning events that it had seemed harmless to tell this woman about it.

They didn't speak again until they pulled up outside the address in Farringdon. The building looked like an office, but it had no indication outside as to what went on behind its black, regal double doors.

'Here we are then,' said Tony, looking back at the woman.

'Thank you,' she said, got out onto the street and waited for him to leave.

Tony pulled away immediately, not wanting to display how uncomfortable he felt. A couple of streets away he took out his little notebook and noted the time, date, pickup and drop off locations and a small description of the woman. He closed his book and wondered what had made him do it.

Back on Farringdon Road, the well-dressed lady watched the cab disappear into the traffic and then quickly pulled a contact up on her phone and rang it.

'Hello, is that Dr Cardolp? It's Dr Matlock. We need to meet this afternoon.' After a brief pause, she continued, 'Yes, it's urgent. I would like you to take me through the full details of the pickup. We have some interesting developments we need to discuss.' There was another brief pause after which Dr Matlock added, '4 pm will be acceptable. Oh and one more thing – I need you to move him into lockdown mode before our meeting at 4 pm.' And with that, Dr Matlock hung up and entered the grand building, kicking angrily at the wooden door as she did so.

Someone was for it.

Chapter 7. Polly & Bert unite

Bert hadn't killed his parents; rationally, he understood this. However, he'd wished them dead too often, and it was this that he couldn't square with himself. At night it haunted him, and when he woke in the morning, his head felt it had been through a grinder of accusations. Taking a bath or buying a bag of oranges, the same shadow followed him around.

Bert was an angry man; he could not forgive his parents for leaving him and when people told him 'everything happened for a reason', he hated them also. Was there a good reason for losing both parents? He supposed he should feel grateful; he knew others who lost their parents much younger, or at birth, or, worse, had parents that didn't care about them. Oh yes, he'd seen every angle, it made no difference. Anger, regrets and ashes piled high.

Their death had been too simple. There was no gruesome murder, death by fire or car crash.

One idle Tuesday, Edith and Scooter Fairwold, as a rare treat and in the act of unusual spontaneity, took an absence of leave. Neither could be certain why, as they were both of the generation that prided themselves on their work ethic. They dropped the kids off to school and agreed they would sit about for a bit, maybe sort out the airing cupboard and recategorise the bookshelf. They engaged in these meaningless tasks for most of the morning when it occurred to Edith that the only thing she wanted to do on her day off was to be taken to bed by her husband and promptly told him so, much to her husband's surprise and delight.

Between kissing, they remembered how much they loved one another. Edith and Scooter talked about the things that made them happy, truly happy; not the usual direct debits, house prices and recycling, but how sometimes listening to a song, watching the rain roll down a window or hearing the other burp, filled them with deep joy.

They spent the rest of the day in a blissful hue. Even the piles of washing and messy bedrooms seemed to be in the perfect place.

Bert had been first out of his class that day. He had been awarded the best prize any self-respecting 13-year-old could ever hope and dream for – the 'Student most likely to go to space' award – and rewarded a VIP pass to the Science Museum, not something to be sniffed at. He knew not to lose his head; this was seriously *big* news.

Leaving the school building, he briefly surveyed the temporary classroom portacabins, beyond which lay the splendidly tempting view of the Limes. The playing fields looked especially green and inviting. He debated the merits of walking through the fields versus catching the bus home, deciding the latter would afford him more people to boast about his prize.

Catching sight of his Mum and Dad's car at the school gates made him immediately hostile. They were always ruining things for Bert. Firstly, there was calling him an older man's name at birth, and now this.

Why were they not at work? Bert never told Edith and Scooter Fairwold that he'd made 'Student most likely to go to space', though, as doting parents, they would have been so proud.

Four years to that day, Skooter died. It was a particularly vicious cancer; thankfully, he didn't suffer too severely. Had it not been for that day, that walk, a trip over a tree root, a visit to A&E and an eventual diagnosis, he wouldn't have seen much of the proceeding four years. It was unnecessary and cruel that Edith died within weeks of Skooter from a heart attack. Her heart was too weak to recover. Four years later, both his parents had stopped existing and been reduced to dust and matter. Nothing was the same again.

Polly walked quickly back to her flat. She checked the time and wondered if she should return to work, but decided it was too late to go back to the office now. She was relieved.

As she neared the flat, she noticed something was a little out of place, or instead, there was something in place that wouldn't usually be there. At her front door was someone dressed for a bad taste party. She upped her pace, and, as she got closer, identified the random.

It was Bert.

She ran towards the door, her mind racing with what to say. She wanted to hug and punch him all at the same time.

'You sodding git, where have you been? What the hell's going on?' she roared in his face and embraced him in an affectionate headlock.

'Ah and there I was hoping you might be lost for words,' said Bert, grinning ear to ear. He was relieved she was cross to see him; she still cared at least.

'I am lost for words. I can't believe you are here. It's been 10 years! I've been looking for you!' Emotions were thick and fast for Polly, who was simultaneously punching and hugging him.

'Ouch cut it out. Where have you been looking for me?' Bert muffled from hiding behind his arms.

'Well actually, I haven't been looking for you, but I was just about to. But first I needed to find Donald. Oh yes, good point, do you know Donald? You must do,' Polly blurted.

'Look, can we just go inside first before the inquisition starts? I'd like to have a cup of tea, and I need the toilet.' Bert looked uncomfortable.

Begrudgingly, Polly let them into the flat. She wondered why he hadn't let himself in. It was, after all, as much his flat as it was hers and she hadn't changed the locks. After fussing about putting the kettle on and turning it off again (Polly had never had got into the swing of buying milk) and Bert dealing with his emergency toilet requirement, they eventually found themselves sitting at the kitchen table.

'So...' Polly looked Bert directly in the eye. She noticed he'd aged a lot, but then again, he was so obviously Bert. Still wearing awful shirts, she thought, eying up the spectacular flamingo covered item.

'I can tell you like my shirt. It was a bargain,' he said.

'By bargain, I assume you mean that you've been paid to wear it. Anything less and you were ripped off,' said Polly, annoyed that he could accurately second-guess her.

'Right, I need to tell you what's been going on. I'm so sorry Polly, I should have come sooner, it was selfish of me.' He looked shamefaced.

'That's OK. Honestly, I was annoyed at first, maybe I still am a little bit. Still, I understand why you had to leave. You were landed a crappy job having to bring me up. You deserved to have your own life,' jumped in Polly with her much-rehearsed line, the one she'd often insisted to friends after several glasses of alcohol.

'It wasn't just that, I needed to get out there and find a reason, or perhaps a purpose, for my own life. I lost my way, I was a 20-something-year-old orphan with no idea what to do or where I was going. I was depressed.' For Polly, who was also a 20-something-year-old orphan, it wasn't a particularly satisfying response. Still, she could at least empathise with him.

'Did you find it?' asked Polly.

'Find what?' Bert looked distant, as if he wasn't paying attention.

Bert, on this occasion, wasn't paying attention to Polly at all. His mind had drifted and he was thinking back to that time in the park with Mum and Dad. Mum had tears in her eyes, he had turned to look at Dad, willing him to conjure up a look of reassurance. The look didn't come. Parks are an excellent place to deliver hard news; there's always a handy bench around fitting for a crisis.

He heard his mum say, 'Your Dad and I have to talk to you about something Bert. We need you to be brave,' in an unusually soft voice. He didn't like her tone; he only ever knew her loud voice or her laughing voice. Bert had been thinking a lot about a boy in his class at school, Simon. He was obsessed with him and his orange jacket. Bert had been trying to work through his feelings about this boy, so he almost missed his mum say, 'It so happens that he's a bit ill, and um...' Bert gave his mum his full attention instantly forgetting about Simon.

'The thing is my boy,' his Dad's voice cut in, 'I'm not at all well. Your Mum's upset, I didn't want her to know, but I cannot hide anything from her. She knows me too well.' Skooter kissed Edith full on the mouth which only served to make Bert pull a face and mockingly wretch. 'We've been talking about my illness. Unfortunately, it's not going to get better. It's terminal.' It was incomprehensible to Bert.

'Your reason or your purpose?' Polly interrupted Bert's thoughts, waving her arms in his face and shouting, 'Are you listening to me?'

'Sorry Pol, yes, yes I'm listening to you. And yes, I did find my purpose. It started shortly after Mum and Dad died, something a bit strange happened. That's the best way I can describe it.' He sat down and pulled his flimsy shirt down to cover his tubby belly.

'Is it to do with the way Mum and Dad died? I've always wondered what went on there.' Polly looked at him suspiciously.

'No Polly, they just died as people do. No big mystery and I'm sorry because I know you've always wanted there to be one, but there isn't anything more to it than that.'

Polly in a small and quiet voice admitted, 'I know, I wish they hadn't though.'

'I know, me too. Perhaps if they hadn't then all...' he stopped and seemed to consider what to say, '...then things would be different. There's no point thinking like that though, it did happen and we have to get on with our lives.'

Rage engulfed Polly. He certainly had got on with his life, leaving her to fend for herself.

After a long pause, Polly regained her calm and said, 'You were young and I don't blame you for going, but 10 years is a long time not to visit.' She looked at him accusingly.

'Yes. It was too long, but the longer I was away, the easier it got. Then it became practically impossible to come back. I wasn't somewhere it was easy to travel from.' Bert looked a bit like a small boy caught experimenting with a box of matches, a mixture of justified annoyance and guilt.

'Where have you been all this time? I got your letters - when you bothered to send them,' she added as a jab at him. Then, seeing his face, reversed tactic. 'Sorry, I mean you never said where you were.'

'If I told you, you wouldn't believe me,' Bert said, not quite looking at her.

Polly gasped and jumped straight to the most logical thing she could think of. 'Were you abducted by aliens?'

'What?' Laughed Bert. 'No, I wasn't abducted by aliens!'

Polly felt annoyed; she didn't think it was that farfetched.

'To be fair though, I did marry one,' Bert concluded.

'Oh OK, yes that makes sense,' Polly said and then reran what he'd just said in her mind. 'No, scrap that, that makes no sense. You did what? You married an alien?!'

'Yes,' said Bert levelly.

'But...you can't have, but...' It was all too much for Polly. She got up and started pacing the room, as if there was an explanation to be had if she moved around a lot.

'I don't think Janet would have liked to have been called an alien, it's a bit...' Bert made a face.

'It's a bit what?' said Polly, looking confused.

'It's a bit racist.' Bert whispered the word racist as if the word itself was rude.

'I am *not* an alien racist,' said Polly, also whispering the word racist. 'I didn't know there even were...' she searched around for a more appropriate name, but couldn't think of one, '... *aliens* here yet. Well, I mean I thought there probably were, it's all the news talks of, but I didn't know.'

'Oh come on Polly.' Bert rolled his eyes at her. 'You mean to tell me you've not encountered any Overs or read anything about them? Have you been living under a rock?'

'No!' she shouted at him, 'And what are *Overs* for crying out loud? Sounds like something to do with cricket.'

'*Overs* is a name for people whose origins are from the planet Overthere. It is also, coincidentally, a set of six balls bowled from one end of a cricket pitch,' he explained, as if talking to a small child of five. 'Please tell me you've at least heard of Overthere? That big, purple planet thing that got in touch a couple of years ago. It was pretty big news Pol.'

Polly knew better than to answer that; she knew he was teasing her. There was so much to take in and ask all at the same time. Purple? Overthere was purple? Well, *that* was new information to her, but she wasn't going to give Bert the satisfaction of looking like an idiot. Somehow, he'd managed to make her feel like the one in the wrong, as if she was the one that had ran away after their parents died and hadn't been in touch for 10 years. She must get better at interrogating him; she hadn't asked him any proper questions yet. She made a small mental note not to become a journalist anytime soon.

'So, Janet is an Over?' she finally asked after a prolonged silence.

'Yes. Well, yes and no,' replied Bert.

'That's cleared things up for me. Thanks,' replied Polly, wondering if Bert would be more or less useful replaced with a chocolate fireguard.

'She's dead now, so yes she was an Over, but now she isn't any more.' Polly cringed at her tactlessness.

'I'm so sorry Bert...I...how did it happen?' Polly spluttered.

'I'd rather not talk about it at the moment, if that's ok. I will, but just not now.' Polly didn't feel she could question him any further on the matter.

Thinking about all the things she could say next that wouldn't sound trite, Bert had wholly withdrawn from the conversation. She'd forgotten his talent for becoming untouchable. She needed to know more, but knew he wasn't going to give her much more to go on right now and he'd put her in a position where she couldn't ask. Damn him.

What do people do in times of awkwardness, in times of grief? What could she possibly do or say to break the silence? Her mind flickered to the day their Mum had died.

'I'm going down the shops for some milk,' she announced. 'Then we can have a lovely cup of tea.'

Bert smiled ruefully and said, 'Polly, put the kettle on.'

In mock annoyance, Polly frowned at him and, as an afterthought, shouted behind her as she made for the door, 'Don't you even *think* about going anywhere! I'll be back in a second.'

Chapter 8. Dr Matlock & Dr Andreas Cardolp

'You're late,' Dr Matlock said, in a tone so full of disdain. Dr Andreas Cardolp wondered if his grandparents' parents hadn't made a massive mistake in daring to cast eyes on each other. He knew from experience that it would be futile to point out that it was just a few minutes past the appointed hour and sat down quickly in front of the large, mahogany desk at which Dr Matlock was lording over.

The large desk gave Dr Matlock an almost elfin appearance, which managed to make her all the more terrifying.

'Good afternoon Dr Matlock. How are you?' he ventured, in a voice he hoped sounded far more confident than he felt. I am a qualified, intelligent, powerful man. He repeated this mantra over and over in his head. He would control this meeting; she was no more important than him. I am a qualified, intelligent, powerful man.

'You have egg mayonnaise on your trousers,' Began Dr Matlock, interrupting his train of thought. 'Update me please.'

Hastily rubbing away the offending egg stain and gathering his papers from his briefcase, he launched into his update.

'Suspect Duck has been captured and is being held securely in the building. We have provided all necessary alibis to his whereabouts. We informed his office of his illegal residency in the UK. We have arranged multiple ongoing payments for all living expenses. Suspect Duck has no known social acquaintances, other than a man by the name of Colin. Colin is a regular drinker at his local pub and would occasionally converse with the suspect on the topic of...' he paused briefly, scouring his notes. Finding the one he was looking for, he continued, 'the colour coding system of salt and vinegar crisp packets.'

'That's not strictly true, is it?' interrupted Dr Matlock.

'Yes it is,' answered Dr Andreas Cardolp, confidently. 'Colin maintains that salt and vinegar crisp packets should be blue, and that cheese and onion should be green. Whereas suspect Duck was ambivalent at best...'

'I'm not talking about fucking crisp packets you incompetent, impotent moron.' Dr Matlock's voice dropped to a quiet hiss.

'Well I, I, I don't think there's any need f...' Dr Andreas began, stuttering in mortified anger.

'I implore you to think very carefully before you answer this next question,' Dr Matlock cut in, drawing back in her chair and licking her lips (the 'cobra position', as it was known internally).

'Do you stand by your assertion that suspect Duck has no other social associates other than this...' she almost spat out the word, 'Colin?'

Dr Andreas Cardolp thought very carefully. He was backed into a corner. His brain tried desperately to second guess why. The unknown reason for the attack was fear-inducing.

'I said suspect Duck has no known social acquaintances other than...'

'Am I to take it you are adopting a plea of incompetence?' Dr Matlock leaned forward in her chair. Strike one.

'I'm not sure I understand,' he offered.

'I am asking you, in your role as Ambassador of Human Concerns of the Official Police, if you believe yourself to be incompetent? Or perhaps that insults your intelligence. Perhaps you are not guilty of incompetence, but instead deliberately providing misleading information. Which is it?'

'It's neither, Dr Matlock. And I don't appreciate this line of interrogation.' Which would have sounded a lot bolder had his voice not quivered quite so dramatically in the middle of it.

'How is it then, that I was first informed of suspect Duck's detainment, not from you, but from a London taxi driver?'

Dr Andreas Cardolp's face grew from bafflement to sheer horror as Dr Matlock updated him on her earlier conversation with Tony, the taxi driver. He wondered if his wife would play his favourite song at his funeral; would she know what it was? Elation passed over him momentarily, as he pondered the merits of his demise. Perhaps death wouldn't be so bad after all. His temporary happiness was postponed as he tuned back into Dr Matlocks voice.

'I want both of them here now,' Dr Matlock barked.

'Um, who?' he asked, lost in his internal conversation.

'Polly and Bert Fairwold.'

'But where will we find Bert Fairwold? We've been looking for a year and Ms Fairwold was never seen as a threat.' He stopped, realising he'd missed a crucial part of the conversation.

'Is it really of any great surprise that Overthere found us first? When people like you are considered to be towards the smart end of the human race,' Dr Matlock said, more to herself than to him.

'Let me just condense this for your tiny, puny mind. Poly Fairwold, is holding the code, is looking for suspect Duck and believes her brother to be involved. She is far more capable than your impact report suggests and puts her second in the threat list, just after her brother.' Her eyes bore deeply into Dr Andreas Cardolp's soul. 'We cannot afford to draw any attention to Ms Fairwold's impending disappearance.' She paused briefly, taking a sip of her coffee that seemed to have appeared from nowhere. 'To be absolutely clear, that means no police and no publicity. If you could also try not to allow any of this knowledge slip to London's taxi network, or accidentally announce it over the radio, that would be splendid.'

'Consider it done,' he managed to muster in his most assertive hamster voice.

'Forgive me if I don't. Get it right and get out of my fucking office. I have an update call with the US, which, thanks to you, is going to go down like a cup of cold Satan shit.' Dr Matloock dismissed him without another word.

Dr Cardolp gathered all his things as quickly as possible and practically ran out of her office. Only to trip over an ill-placed rug and, to his mortification, let out a, hopefully unnoticeable, trouser parp. A glance behind him at Dr Matlock's flint-like look of disgust, confirmed that stealth was still lingering at the bottom of his ever-dwindling list of talents.

Chapter 9. Teatime theme time

Have you ever tried to tell a British person there's no milk for their tea? We do not recommend it. It'll break your heart as you watch their little, beady faces start to comprehend the full gravity of the situation. It is the angriest you will *ever* see a British person. It's crucial to remember not to mention anything that tips them over the edge. Understand that this person currently hates you and thinks you are a moron. Expect phrases like, 'No I don't want lemon,' and, 'I hate lemons, lemons are stupid.'

No sooner as Polly reached the oak tree halfway up the road to the high street, she realised that it might have been a stupid idea to leave Bert in the house on his own. What if he disappears again? she thought to herself. She stopped just outside the garage with the ominous 'Madagascar' neon sign. Should she go back? But then, if he hadn't left, she'd be back in the house with no milk for tea. Damn it, she thought to herself. Why didn't she think before she acted? She became aware that there was some movement inside the garage and a strange-looking man with a humongous, red beard was peering out at her.

Staring back at him, unsure if she should go in and pretend she needed the garage services. Polly had always assumed it was a garage; on closer inspection, she realised that she'd never seen a car in the forecourt and the petrol pumps didn't even have nozzles. Turning away, confused and a bit frightened of the man with the big red beard, she ran towards the shops.

On her return, she took a more extended look at the garage and slowed up her pace. There were no signs to suggest what services were on offer. Perhaps it was some sort of drugs den. Then she noticed the man with the red beard again stood outside, a little way back off the street. He was still watching her and Polly felt unnerved as she came to pass him. She thought she'd heard him say something and whipped back around.

'Pardon?' Polly said, her voice taking on her best middle-class pitch.

The red-bearded man looked at her a little startled.

'Sorry did you say something?' she asked again.

The man continued to look at her in a fascinated fashion, leaned in towards her and semi-whispered, 'We didn't expect you so soon?'

'What do you mean?' she asked, puzzled.

He suddenly composed himself and said, 'Nothing.' The way he said it seemed to imply something.

She looked at him again. He was pretty big and scaring looking, plus potentially out of his mind.

'OK, good, good stuff. Bye then.' She gave a little wave and scurried off back to the flat.

Polly was relieved to see Bert's shoes in the hall. He was still here, thank goodness.

Chapter 10. The search for Donald

Polly and Bert sat across from each other, sipping their pints of cider in the Worm and Duck. After two cups of tea, a sandwich and endless talks about the weather, they had sensibly concluded that the pub was the best course of action.

'They've got rid of the fruit machine,' Bert commented.

'I don't want to go into the ins and outs of the pub's interior design, if that's alright,' replied Polly. 'I'd like to know how you know Donald. I take it you do know him?' she asked.

'Yes, I do know him.' Bert shuffled uncomfortably in his seat.

'And is he a... an Over?' Polly corrected herself quickly.

'Yes, I believe he is. I met him a couple of years ago, when I was doing some building work for a finance company. We got chatting outside one day. I can't remember what it was about, something to do with the Moon I think.'

'So, you've been in London then?' blurted out Polly, trying and failing not to react to the painful realisation he'd been so close to her.

'Yes. Not the whole time. I came back when...I came back a few years ago.'

'Where have you been living? Why didn't you get in touch?' The bitterness was impossible to hide; the cider loosened her tongue.

'I told you, it was difficult and I was trying to keep a low profile. I didn't want to get you mixed up in things.' Bert paused. Polly gave him a look.

'What type of things?' Polly was getting frustrated.

'Believe me when I tell you, you shouldn't know the types of things I was involved with,' he said.

'If you told me you'd have to kill me, heh?' Polly scoffed.

'I can just as easily kill you without telling you anything, if you want to go on taking the piss.' It was Bert's turn to look annoyed now.

'OK, OK. Tell me about Donald and this code,' she urged, changing the topic.

Bert looked at her sharply. Polly wondered what on earth she'd said to annoy him now.

'What do you mean "this code"?' Bert said.

'The code that you gave Donald to give to me,' she replied.

'I didn't give Donald a code to give to you. I gave him a letter to pass on to you, to let you know I was safe and I'd be coming to see you soon.' Bert's eyes flickered for a nanosecond.

'That's not what he gave me. He gave me this code that would give me the answer to everything or something.' Polly couldn't remember exactly the words Donald had used.

'He did what? What was he playing at? This is not the plan. He was supposed to just pop round and see that you were OK, that was all, I swear.' Bert paused to take a sip of his pale, gold drink, pulling a face. 'So what's this code then?'

Polly fumbled in her bag and pulled out the now crumpled paper, bringing with it an elastic band a few crumbs.

Bert carefully unwrapped the paper and read it aloud. He seemed frozen for a moment, then visibly relaxed and even ventured a smile. 'Where is he now?'

'I don't know where he is. I was going to ask you that. You're telling me you don't know?'

Polly explained the last 24 hours to him with as much detail as she could remember, leaving nothing out – Donald calling round the flat, her morning adventures, Tony the taxi driver, going to Donald's office, the lot.

Bert returned from the bar with the fourth pint of cider for them both. He sat back and rubbed his chin. 'Did you think to go around to his house?' he asked.

'And how exactly am I supposed to know where that is? No, I didn't go to his house. I have no idea where he lives, do you know?'

'Yes, he lives somewhere in Vauxhall.'

'Well, let's get down there now,' Polly hiccupped, then lightly burped.

Bert checked the time. 'I think it might be a bit late tonight. I don't know the exact address. We need a proper plan and,' he added disapprovingly, 'you're drunk.'

'No I bloody well am not,' she hiccupped again. 'OK, I might be a tiny bit. Let's forget about it tonight. Here's the plan, tomorrow morning, the first thing we do is find Donald's house!'

'I don't think we can stay here tonight.' Bert's face had become serious again. Polly hated this stern face; where had it come from? It was never there before, or if it was he'd never used it. 'We need to go somewhere safe where we can think. It's too late to go to Donald's and...' He went to say something else but thought the better of it. 'We'll go to mine. We'll get some rest, make sure we get up early and waste no time.'

'Yes, yes, we will. I'll set my alarm for 5 am, then we'll get to the bottom of this.' Polly paused, leaning back on her chair. For a moment she checked herself. She was back in the Worm and Duck with her brother, her brother who she'd presumed dead on several occasions.

Getting up from her chair and picking up her purse, she smiled at him. 'What shot do you want?'

Chapter 11. They know where you live

Hi Steve,

Unfortunately, I will not be in the office today as I am dealing with a family crisis. If you need anything urgently, please call. I hope to be back in the office on Monday.

Cheers, Polly.

P.S. Kelly has the file you need for the London summit meeting; it's all up to date.

> *Hi Polly,*
>
> *I hope you feel better soon.*
>
> *P.S. Are you able to join the conference call tomorrow (Friday)?*
>
> *Thanks, Steve.*

Hi Steve,

Thanks, I will endeavour to join the call tomorrow. Unfortunately, due to a family crisis, I can't commit to this, but feel free to call if you need anything.

KR, Polly.

OK.

Thanks, Steve

The agonising pain inside Polly's skull receded momentarily to celebrate her cunning at getting out of work for the next four days. She'd probably have to work twice as hard and long next week, but that was next week's problem; for now, she was free. If it was possible to hop out of a sofa bed, then Polly got close to doing it.

Bert's flat reminded Polly of a TV programme she'd seen about extreme weather, where a tornado had devastated a community, leaving behind broken bits of furniture, upturned trees and clutter, only less organised.

It infuriated her that all this time he'd been hiding out here in Stockwell, less than half an hour away from her apartment. It was a miracle they hadn't bumped into each other.

She was up before him and hunting for a container to have a glass of water. Giving up, she opted for a swig from the tap. She wished she were back in her flat in Putney.

Slowly, current events caught up with her and her joy slowly evaporated. What was Bert so afraid of? Why had they come to his flat to hide? From whom were they hiding?

She aimlessly wandered around, picking up objects and strange things around her. She went to the bookcase, interested to see if there was anything to distract her. She was surprised to find several children's books scattered among self-help books and a few sporting biographies, with names such as *Born to Cycle* and *I Can Move Any Mountain Bike*. It's funny how people change, thought Polly, recalling Bert's aversion to getting on a bicycle. The children's books baffled her the most; he'd not mentioned any children. Her eyes fell to a small, pocket-sized book with a dark, battered cover entitled *Mentor Tome*. She took it down from the shelf and was mesmerized by the shiny, gold imprinted letters and the elaborately decorated planet on the cover. Now, this was something she wanted to read and absent-mindedly tucked it away in her bag. As she did this, the piece of paper Donald had given her, not 48 hours earlier, dropped to the floor.

She opened it up again and looked uncomprehendingly at the code.

       www.nothing.com

What the hell did it mean? She thought back to her plan of action. Searching around a pile of debris, she found an abandoned letter and a broken crayon on Bert's kitchen table. She sat down to update her list.

1. Find Donald
2. Find Bert
3. Find out what I want

Well, she'd found Bert, or he'd found her, so that was a tick off the list. She would have to wait until Bert woke up to figure out how to find Donald. So that just left 'Find out what I want'.

Oh, just that small question. What do I want? She wondered.

There were, of course, hundreds of things that Polly wanted. She started to make a list.

> Miniature indoor fireworks
> ~~A pet pigeon – but only if the pigeon wants to be my pet~~
> A pigeon as a friend
> Yellow trainers
> A nice fountain pen with a bendy nib
> Green towels
> A new keyring
> Some paints – must be oil paints
> Travel scrabble

She stopped and revisited her list, apart from the pigeon friend they were all material things that she could quite easily acquire herself. She felt she wasn't thinking big enough. She started a new list, this time she named it BIG stuff I want

> World Peace and social justice
> ~~Resolution to the housing crisis~~
> Humane resolution to the housing crisis
> ~~Protection of the environment~~
> Adequate protection of the environment
> Establish new planet for human habitation

She reviewed the big list. Her mind boggled; this list was too big. When she thought about it, she wasn't even sure what most of it would entail. Take world peace, for a start – some people love having a row, so if they stopped rowing would they be at peace? She carried this thought down a vast, black hole of confusing paradoxes.

OK, come on Polly, you can do this. She mentally picked herself off the proverbial floor again. What do you want? What was missing from her life? With a quick look over her shoulder, she scribbled down:

> For Bert to stay

And then even smaller underneath:

> ...A boyfriend?

A warm rush flooded to her cheeks as tears threatened to prick her eyes but quickly shoved away. Overwhelmed and mentally paralysed, her hangover returned. The desire to lie down was intense.

Bert walked into the kitchen wearing just his pants and a T-shirt with 'How soon is now?' embossed on it. He had also creatively decorated the T-shirt with a luminous yellow dye.

> 'You ooze class,' said Polly sarcastically, before vomiting a little in her mouth.

After rushing to the bathroom, she returned, slightly grey and shaky. Ignoring her, Bert had produced a shiny, new laptop from somewhere and was busy typing away.

'What now?' said Polly.

'We have to find Donald,' said Bert, taking charge.

'Please tell me what's going on first,' pleaded Polly. 'This is all so strange.'

Bert sighed and shut his laptop. 'OK, but you need to listen and not make stupid jokes.'

The urge to make a stupid joke was unbearable, however, Polly held her tongue and nodded at him to go on.

'I needed to find out what I wanted from life. I was unhappy and felt suffocated. Every day that passed, it became harder to come back. I felt bad. I know you needed me, but I couldn't do it. I couldn't be your rock when I was falling apart myself. I told myself I'd done you a favour. I'd left you the flat and enough money…' He looked away as if hearing his feebleness.

'It's OK, I forgive you,' said Polly matter-of-factly. And as with anyone who'd ever uttered those words before translated to, I haven't forgiven you.

'Then, I met Janet. She was so different from everyone else I'd ever met her before. I met her in a therapy group for overcoming anxiety. I fell in love with her. At first, everything was a dream. We got married one

New Year's Eve, on a whim. But it felt so right.' He looked away dreamily. 'She wanted to meet you. We almost did once, but I was too ashamed. I wanted to pretend I was a good bloke, not the type of bloke that would abandon his orphaned sister.' He looked at her, willing her to understand.

'Things changed rapidly after contact from Overthere, Janet became distant and preoccupied. Eventually, she told me that she was an Over. It was a complete shock at first and I didn't really believe her. But as the months passed, it began to make sense and then it became routine. I was naturally fascinated by her heritage, I wanted to tell the world, I became obsessed with her race, but Janet hated it. I didn't realise her entire mission was to find our similarities, the things that made us the same, the things that bind our races together. I was looking for every difference, comparing us and celebrating her superiority. Perhaps subconsciously I was overcompensating. I believed her to be better, but I patronised and belittled her without knowing. I thought I was open-minded.'

As Polly listened, she noted it was the first time she had heard him sound so truthful and vulnerable. Before her eyes, he became a small boy again with a washing up bowl on his head. Her heart softened.

Bert's face became angry. 'Jealousy came next. I felt I wasn't good enough for her. She was an Over and had travelled to Earth from Overthere. Did she see other Overs behind my back?' He paused and looked to Polly. Polly remained silent.

After a short time, he continued. 'Janet realised very quickly that my behaviour would be similar to that of all earthlings and that fascination would lead to suspicion. When she told me she was feeling trapped, I told her she was paranoid.' He stopped and raised his hands to his head, gripping his hair.

'What happened? How did she die?' Polly felt uneasy and sick again, because somewhere in her consciousness she thought she already knew.

'She was missing for two weeks before I received a visit from the Official Police saying she was found dead. The verdict was suicide.'

'And was it?' ventured Polly.

'No, it was not. They killed her.' Bert's face turned hard and unreadable.

'Who? Who killed her?' Polly was confused.

'The Official Police,' Bert snarled.

Polly snorted with laughter. Everyone knew the story behind the Official Police. A few years ago, when social media was taking over the world, a criminal gang registered the username for every police unit in the UK. Once the group had been found out, they refused to hand over the usernames, and therefore the Police were forced to set up a division called the Official Police, to match their name and to forever be mocked as such.

Bert looked at her deadly serious. 'I take it you haven't had a lot of dealing with the Official Police? They are not some urban myth from the internet Polly. They were set up by the Home Office as soon as Overthere contacted us. It's their job to identify, arrest and kill every alien in the UK.'

'They cannot be allowed to kill people. It sounds like a conspiracy theory to me.' Polly was feeling confused. She couldn't believe what he was telling her.

'I know what it sounds like, and no they are not allowed to kill humans. But there's nothing to stop them killing aliens – *they* have no rights, *they* are deemed a threat. The Official Police can do whatever they want.' He gripped the arm of his chair so tightly Polly that saw all the veins protrude from his hands.

Polly decided to humour him.

'And you think the Official Police have Donald too?'

'I do now I know he's given you the code,' replied Bert earnestly. 'Don't you have any idea what's happening Polly?' He looked directly at her as if he could make her believe him if he stared for long enough.

'Can you imagine how we are responding? Earth is no longer top dog. Panic is rife at the highest levels. People who thought they were the most powerful people in the universe now feeling stupid and weak. They want to root out all the Overs and destroy Overthere. They want their positions in the universe and their power back.'

'But why?' Polly asked.

'Because numbnuts, they are suspicious and scared. Have you heard the rumours that Overthere wants to take over Earth?' said Bert.

'No! Do they really?' asked Polly, wide-eyed.

'No, they don't. That's what I'm telling you. Can't you see it? Earth wants us to believe that Overthere is planning to attack us to justify destroying it.' He gave her a beseeching look. 'OK fine, don't believe me.' He walked over to the TV and put on the 24-hour news. Polly would have preferred it if he'd invited a band of howling foxes into the house, rather than watch crappy, rolling, pointless, echo chamber news.

He tried a different tact. 'It's not your fault Polly, you have been duped, we all have. They are going to destroy everything.'

Polly was gradually drawn into the news clips going round and round:

> 'Inevitable war with Overthere.'
> 'Do you know your neighbour?'
> 'How much are Overthere paying in tax?'
> 'Human murdered by alien.'
> 'Alien terrorist group detained.'

'Overthere have potential to arm nuclear bombs.'

'Oh,' said Polly. 'Why though? What's the point? I don't get it.' She felt an overwhelming sense of impending doom. 'How are we going to get Donald back?'

'Don't know.' They both sat transfixed by the endless rolling of fear stories filling the screen.

Suddenly Polly sat up straight. 'I've got an idea!' she said excitedly.

'What is it?' Bert asked cautiously.

'Where's the best place to hide?'

'I'm not up for a game Polly,' said Bert, annoyed.

'It's not a game. Where is the best place to hide? Where everyone can see you!' she exclaimed proudly, nodding towards the TV.

Chapter 12. Public appeal

Air Studios stood high and mighty on the Kings Road. Bert shifted around in his best suit, clearly uncomfortable.

'Have you got it then?' Polly asked him.

'I still don't know why I have to wear a suit,' he said grumpily.

'No one will believe that you're important otherwise.'

'Are you sure this is going to work?' Bert asked nervously.

'I'm as sure as a royal wandering around a minefield for a photoshoot.' Polly attempted some humour to distract him.

'What does that even mean? Was that supposed to be a joke?' Bert looked puzzled.

'Forget it. No I'm not sure, but we haven't got anything better.' Polly hurriedly pushed Bert into position.

She took out the rolled-up bedsheet onto which they had painted in big red letters 'My husband has been abducted by aliens'.

'Now what?' Bert looked about nervously.

'Now we have to have a row and, hopefully, that will be enough bait for the news reporters at Air to become interested.'

'Why the hell did I let you talk me into this?' Bert cried.

Annabel 'Aces' Jones was bored with the bulletin she was trying to write; it only required a brief outline of the pros and cons of capitalism. She may as well have been asked to translate the Bible into a microwave. After several attempts of trying to engage the man sat on the desk opposite her in light conversation and refilling the toner on the printer, she gave up and awarded herself a five-minute respite of looking out the window. The Air offices, that she once considered glamorous, back when she was a fresh-blooded human journalist, still held the one redeeming feature of having windows, so you could dream of escaping.

Looking down at all the tiny bug-people milling around below, she became instantly interested in a big, red banner and two people alongside it. From the look of the arm gestures, the couple was either arguing or practising an elaborate message in semaphore. The headline on the banner caught her eye.

'Hey Geoff,' she said, excitely motioning to the disinterested desk colleague. 'Come and look at this, that couple are having a massive barney down there.'

Geoff, having been interrupted for the umpteenth time from trying to download the online game *Civilisation ExtraTerrestrial XX* decided to humour Aces Jones, hoping that, if he spoke to her for five minutes, perhaps she'd leave him alone for the rest of the day. A plan that had never previously proven to work.

'Look, she's trying to get him in a headlock,' said Aces, as if Geoff was not witnessing the same thing.

There is a widespread behaviour in offices when people are trying to find anything else to do but work. In the space of 30 seconds, half the news desk and a couple of the finance team were all bunched around the windows watching the argument unfold.

'Quick, let's get down there and film it.' Shouted one bright spark. The crowd mutually agreed it was the only thing to do.

'Do you think aliens have abducted her husband?' said another.

It was all the encouragement Aces Jones and a camera crew required.

Polly clocked the camera before Bert. 'They're coming over,' she whispered to him waiting for them to get in earshot before shouting, 'I KNOW THE GOVERNMENT IS TRYING TO HUSH IT UP.'

It was Bert's cue to run off. Aces Jones and the camera team hurried to Polly.

'Are you OK? What's happening here?' Aces thrust a mic under Polly's chin.

'Aliens have abducted my husband, and that man,' Polly pointed to Bert, who was now halfway up the road, '*that* man is from the government and he's trying to hush it up.'

'Really?! Wow, how exciting, I mean, how *awful* for you,' exclaimed Aces Jones, who aimed to muster up empathy, but delivered it with the accuracy of an England footballer lining up to take the fourth penalty in the quarter-final of any popular tournament. 'Why don't you come inside and talk to us about it? We can put out an appeal for you.' Aces mouthed to Steph, the researcher, 'Get that man – the one in that awful suit.'

Polly followed Aces Jones into a studio where she was dusted, wired and shoved on a watermelon that was, not so cleverly, disguised as a sofa.

Within 30 minutes, Polly's pleading face beamed out around the world. She and her fictitious husband received empathic messages from enthused members of the public. Sightings of the abduction flooded in.

As Polly predicted, Ace Jones, having achieved her story, had booted her back out of the Air offices and arranged a taxi to pick her up. A small huddle of sad and grey reporters gathered around the main entrance, so she was bundled into the black beacon of mercy from a side street and it took her a few minutes to recognise who was driving.

'Tony. It's you!' Polly was never so happy to see a friendly face.

'Hello Polly love, what a turn up for the books. It seems I can't get rid of you.' He grinned his genial, big face at hers through the mirror. 'Lemme just get us out of this street. I'm pleased I've met you again. Something strange happened after I picked you up before.' He broke off as he single-handedly outmanoeuvred a bus and several pedestrians.

'Oh Tony, can we pick up my brother? I told him to wait near the station?' she asked, quickly remembering this part of the plan.

'Sure thing, you found him then? I knew you would.' He pulled the cab up into a small parking bay round the corner of Kings Cross and turned off the engine while Polly navigated Bert to safety.

Back in the cab, all of them had something to say and tried to speak at once. Polly won the battle, quickly blabbing out all that had happened from when she'd last seen Tony – Bert turning up, staying at his flat, discovering Bert was married, Janet's disappearance and death, the plan to find Donald and the TV interview. Bert nodded along and added his pieces of information, correcting Polly when she made up bits that she couldn't remember.

Tony sighed and leaned back in his seat, resting his hands on his knees as if meditating in thought. Polly and Bert watched him eagerly in wait for whatever it was he was going to say next.

'What about the other thing? The genie?' he said cryptically, turning to look at Polly.

Oh great, he's lost his marbles she thought, but said nothing out-loud, instead leaning in a little to search for clues in his mapped face.

'The *genie*,' he said again, nodding his head slightly and blatantly winking.

It clicked. 'Oh you mean the code? It's OK, Bert knows about the code,' she said quickly, as Tony inexpertly made signals that she might want to remain aloof on the matter. 'Funny you should mention that as we haven't sussed that out at all, have we Bert?' It wasn't really a question, and Polly continued, 'It wasn't anything to do with Bert. I'm not sure it's anything to do with anything.'

'Hmm,' said Tony, rubbing his chin. He'd noticed something Polly hadn't, and that was how quiet Bert had gone; his face was masked, quite literally, by his hands.

'Have you thought about what you want if it turned out to be real? Just in case.'

Polly thought back to her small, big and secret list, but could only remember something about being friends with a pigeon and the boyfriend. It was right, she was still keen on both those ideas, but there was not a chance she was saying that aloud.

'Well I'm not sure, it's probably just some big joke. I mean, it can't be real anyway because it's just a bit of paper. How could it possibly be anything but a joke?' asked Polly, more to herself than anyone.

'My wife has a saying.' Tony looked around at Polly. 'She says, "Tony, you gotta know what you want out of life."' He sat back to allow Polly to absorb these pearls of wisdom fully.

Polly sat looking at him, waiting for the concluding line that didn't follow. 'That's not exactly a saying as such,' she said.

'It's the best one you're going to get. What she *means* is, if you don't know what you want, then how would you know how to get it?'

Polly continued to look at him blankly. 'A saying is usually something a little more rhythmical and less literal than that. Like, "don't count your chickens before they've hatched", or "too many chefs spoil the broth."'

'That's not getting the baby boiled,' chimed in Bert.

Polly stopped and turned to him. 'That's not a saying either. You're not helping.'

'When in Rome, do unto others as they will undo to you,' he continued.

'That doesn't make any sense. Bert, what you're saying doesn't make sense. Can you shut up? Anyway, what is your point, Tony?' Polly pressed him.

'My point is love, maybe it's worth thinking about the question anyway. If this is a joke, there is no harm in thinking about what you want from life, is there? Is there something you want to do with your life? Is there something you want?' Tony impatiently tapped the steering wheel.

Polly gazed out at the world moving around her – all the cars, dust and people. What on earth was it all about anyway? Why was she here? What did she want? What was the point? Didn't everyone die in the end? Wasn't that the punchline of all this? A sort of weird joke. Was there anything else? Looking up to the sky, she noticed a huge, white cloud in the shape of a mushroom.

Words are beautiful things, almost musical. The sound of them can augment everything around you into beats, tones, sounds and heart thumps. But they still didn't capture everything; they couldn't substitute that cloud at that moment. Language was a struggle, a struggle to express something that, the more you explained it, the more you thought about it, the further away it got.

An epiphany is an experience of sudden and striking realisation. Tony had well and truly hit the nail on the head.

Lots of people can tell you something, but it doesn't mean anything to you. Friends and loved ones can say to you over and over again, and it barely registers. Then, one day, when your brain is open to the information, or in this case distracted by a comparative stranger who will say exactly what everyone else has been trying to tell you for years, and all of a sudden it clicks. 'Yes!', you think. 'Why haven't I thought of it like that before? It makes perfect sense.'

What had Polly been doing with life before Donald knocked on her door just a few nights previous? Sure, she had friends, chores and a job to keep her busy, but in many respects she'd been waiting for something. In truth, Polly hadn't done a great deal in her life.

Polly thought through her previous aspirations and remembered wanting to get a job where she got to sit in a chair that swivelled around. As a child, Polly had wanted to be either an actor or someone who ironed clothes. An actor, because she enjoyed making things up and someone who ironed clothes, because the iron was off-limits to her and therefore seemed like the most exciting thing in the universe.

Thinking back to her small, big and secret list, the things on her big list were out of her control, and she wasn't sure how much she wanted the stuff on her little list. They were only accessories; after all, they wouldn't change her life. If Bert would stay, he'd drive her crazy. And a boyfriend seemed too...too small. Her heart did a little leap.

Tony's voice became audible to her once more. 'You don't have to solve it now, you just have to think about it. There's no rush, you just take your time, so long as you do think about it, Polly.'

'There is one thing I do want to do,' she exclaimed, 'get hold of Donald. I'm worried that something is going to happen to him.' She thought back to what Bert had said.

'Do you know where he might be? Did you manage to get his home address?' Tony addressed Polly. He was concerned about that man Bert. He couldn't put his finger on why, but he'd always been a pretty good judge of character and his instinct was seldom wrong.

'Somewhere in south London, but we don't know exactly where. It looks like we're stuck. Maybe we have to head home and see if the appeal helps.'

'Oh!' exclaimed Tony, making them both jump. 'I didn't tell you, did I?'

'What?' Bert and Polly said simultaneously.

'Well the last time I dropped you off, after we popped to the pub, I went back on a shift and, low and behold, I got a pick up from the Hurlingham Club. Some woman, from all angles she was a tiny thing, but a bit frightening,' he laughed quickly. 'You know, she was just one of those stern-looking types, no smiles from her. So anyway, I picked her up, and I suppose I was a little excited after our morning, so, just to break the silence, I started to tell her about our little escapade. I can't say why, but I felt that she was too keenly interested. I think she took some notes, in a way I was not supposed to see. It might be nothing, but I've got a good sense for these things. Comes with the job see. She asked me to repeat Donald's name. I pretended to forget because I was suspicious.' Tony shuffled a bit in his seat.

'That's so strange. Who did you think she was?' Polly was wide-eyed.

'I don't know. I was so suspicious, that I wrote down the address I'd dropped her at, so I wouldn't forget.' He went on, 'These things,' indicating to the dashboard of the taxi cab, 'keep all information about where I'm going and what I'm getting paid, so I didn't need to write anything down. It turns out it was a good job I did, though, because later, when I tried to find a record of the trip via the GPS, it had disappeared completely. Although I still got paid for the fare.' He rubbed his chin meaningfully.

'They can change all forms of digital records,' piped up Bert.

'Who can?' Tony asked, puzzled.

Bert seemed to be weighing up something. 'Nothing, don't worry,' he interjected quickly.

'Have you still got the address?' Polly leaned up to the dividing glass.

'I do actually.' Tony produced a piece of paper from his top pocket.

'I think we should go and suss it out,' she said, eyeing the paper.

'Are you insane?' Bert roared at her, taking her by surprise.

'What's the matter?'

'Have you listened to anything I've been telling you? We can't go to them.' Bert looked like a wild animal for a moment. As if someone had drawn extra lines on his face, she could see his skull under his skin.

'Why not? If it is *them*, then we can find out if they have Donald. And if it's not them, well, no harm done. It's not as if we've got anywhere better to go.' Polly waited for Bert to respond as he sat in silence, calculating his form of mathematics.

'Well we could at least go there I suppose, but you've got to take this seriously Polly.'

Tony watched the pair of them. Unnoticed, he saw the two sides of the same coin and wondered was it was about Bert that he struggled to understand. Where Polly was light, Bert was dark. He was so serious, that one.

'I will. I am taking this seriously,' Polly corrected herself, trying to put on a face that she thought looked more serious. 'Tony, what do you think?'

'I think we should go and suss it out. What have we got to lose?' he said evenly.

'Agreed. Let's do it.' Quickly, before Bert could back out, Tony turned on the engine of the black beast and swung them around. Bert was about to protest again, but thought the better of it and sunk back into his thoughts. Polly felt her phone buzz for the 80th time with messages from friends and people she'd met on workshops. Having seen the broadcasted appeal, they'd been sending her messages, some asking her, understandably, who the hell Donald was and when was she going to tell them she'd got married. Bugger, she hadn't thought about that, that her friends might see the broadcast. Hmm, no time to worry about that now, it was a problem for later.

The newest message was from her boss, Steve. It read:

> Hi Polly,
>
> We're all thinking of you and your husband at this difficult time.
>
> Love, Steve.
>
> P.S. Don't worry about the conference call.

What conference call?

Chapter 13. Polly & Bert meet the officials

Polly and Bert walked past 49 Farringdon Road several times before identifying it. Tony had regretfully been called home, but left them with an insistence that Polly rang him later. The majestic, red-brick building stood numberless in a row of shabby shops. It was almost rendered invisible by its imposing neighbour, a brown slab of concrete making a poor impression of a delightful place to work.

At street level, the narrow, arched windows dressed in white slats, obscured any sign of what went on behind its jet-black double doors.

Polly remembered the solicitors' offices she'd attended for the reading of her parents' will. The buzzer was unmarked; when pressed, the intercom crackled to life. No one spoke or asked any questions. A sharp beep indicated the door had allowed them access; they pushed through and stepped into an eerie, empty reception with a vast staircase.

They both looked around wondering what to do next, when two men and a woman ascended the stairs. The woman, dressed immaculately in a perfectly tailored, dark suit, spoke first as they reached the bottom of the red-carpeted steps.

'Ms Polly Fairwold, Mr Bert Fairwold, we'd like you to follow us please.' She offered no handshake and spoke sternly. Polly was reminded of her deputy headmistress and checked if her shirt was tucked in, then remembered she wasn't wearing one.

'Sorry, but may I just...' began Polly.

'Thank you, yes of course,' Bert interrupted, kicking Polly on the ankle, knowing that whatever was going to come from his sister's mouth wouldn't move things along.

They walked quickly down a corridor with impossibly high ceilings. Birds-eye sketches of areas in London covered the walls interspersed with portraits of people. Polly had never seen these portrait-people before, yet recognised them as powerful, with their all-knowing faces. The lighting was soft and had a feel of a very grand hotel or members club.

They entered a room set out like a living room, where there were two large sofas and a coffee table with a tea service laid out. Polly eyed-up the biscuits. No chocolate hobnobs here.

'Please sit down,' said the dark-tailor-suited-woman. 'We have a lot to discuss. I don't think you need me to tell you that you are both in a very...negative situation.'

Polly couldn't help it and let out a little squeak of a laugh, that earned her a stern look from all present, including Bert.

'My name is Dr Matlock. I am the Ambassador of Knowledge for the Official Police.'

Dr Matlock indicated with her head towards the taller man. 'This is Mr Luc Smith, my Executive Assistant, and Dr Andreas Cardolp,' she nodded at the man now sitting in an oversized armchair, 'Ambassador of Human Concerns.' Polly felt the overwhelming urge to giggle.

'We'd like you to answer some of our questions.' Polly and Bert exchanged a look.

'We have a few questions ourselves,' Polly ventured boldly. 'We haven't done anything wrong. All we want to know is where our friend Donald is.' She mentally put quotation marks around the term *friend*.

'How interesting that you refer to Donald as your friend Ms Fairwold. Can you tell me the exact nature of your relationship?'

'What do you mean?' asked Polly. 'Donald is our friend. Isn't he Bert?'

'I'm talking to you Ms Fairwold, not Mr Fairwold. What is the true nature of your relationship with Donald? Is he not your husband?' Dr Matlock's eyes bore into Polly.

'Well. I mean we're friends, and lovers,' stuttered Polly, mortified having used the word 'lovers' in front of this woman.

'I see. I'm going to need something a little more specific. Let's start with how long you have known Donald Pigeon.'

Polly realised that she'd have to tell the truth, as it was clear to her that Dr Matlock knew the answer anyway. 'Well, the truth is I only met him a few days ago.' Polly wondered why this felt like a lie. Her relationship with Donald was more profound than that. Having devoted the last few days looking for him, she'd grown close to him and yet it was only her side of it, not his. Feeling stupid, she anticipated the next question.

'This great friend of yours, the one you raised a public appeal for, much to the ridicule of the Official Police, you met for the first time three days ago? And how many times since that seemingly all-important meeting have you met since?' Dr Matlock almost smiled.

'Well, it was just that one time, but I think, well I know, a little more about him now and...' Polly stopped herself. She could hear how stupid she sounded out loud; it was bloody stupid. Something suddenly occurred to Polly, but she needed to think. If the Official Police knew she didn't know Donald, why were they asking her questions? What on earth could they want? It started to dawn on Polly that the whole thing was decidedly fishy. The Official Police had been expecting them.

'I must say Ms Fairwold, you do seem to attach very little to what you consider a friendship. Do you count all people you meet once a *friend*? You must find it difficult to keep up with birthdays.' If this was a joke, then it was well hidden.

Polly noticed that Bert was unusually quiet. She turned to glance at him. It was strange, he looked in control, not scared or moved in any way. It was also odd that he hadn't mentioned his friendship with Donald. Something else was clear, though she was the one being questioned and shamed, all three members of the Official Police were looking at Bert.

'You also say that you have done nothing wrong. Now that's not true, is it Mr Fairwold?'

Bert said nothing. Polly turned to look at him and felt unnerved. He remained silent.

'What do you mean?' she asked eventually.

'Please let Mr Fairwold answer.' Dr Matlock's eyes glinted at Bert.

'Let's start with something easier. Where have you been for the last few years Mr Fairwold?'

Still, Bert didn't make any move to answer her.

'Not keen to answer, I see. How did you first meet Janet Planet?'

Bert barely moved, his eyes flickered briefly to Polly and back to Dr Matlock. A movement noted by all.

'Who on earth is Janet Planet? Is that your wife, Janet? *Janet*, Janet?' asked Polly to Bert.

Bert's face took on a strange quality, a glassy-eyed distance, he looked almost waxy.

'She is no one on *Earth* Ms Fairwold,' answered Dr Matlock.

'I would like a lawyer,' said Bert.

'Ah I'm afraid that won't be possible Mr Fairwold. You gave up that right when you actively chose to take part in interplanetary terrorism,' Mr Andreas Cardolp spoke up for the first time. He had a slight hint of malice in his voice, enjoying, for once, not being the object of Dr Matlock's scorn.

'Interplanetary terrorism? What's that?' Polly felt things had moved on several paces; she was drifting behind, trying to catch up.

'*The Interplanetary Terrorism Bill* was set up shortly after the planet Overthere discovered Earth. We correctly predicted that there was a deeper reason for contact between the two planets than mere neighbourly interest. Your brother, Ms Fairwold, is fully aware of that.' Mr Andreas Cardolp warmed to his subject. 'Simply put, Overthere are planning to invade Earth, and your brother here is leading the crusade.'

'Please!' interrupted Dr Matlock, her voice pricked into Cardolp's spine. 'Stick to the facts. It's exactly that sort of simplistic reasoning that has put us all in this situation.'

'What situation?...What are you talking about? Why would Overthere want to attack Earth?' Polly was wholly baffled. She tried to understand but couldn't calculate it. Who was telling the truth here? Everyone contradicted each other.

'You might not like it Dr Cardolp,' continued Dr Matlock, ignoring Polly, 'but Overthere developed far more superior space technology than we on Earth could dare dream of. We are way behind in this so-called race. We are a threat only to ourselves, as uncomfortable and as small as that might make us feel. We are too insignificant for Overthere to attack.'

'Well, we believe Overthere wants the rich resources the Earth offers and our jobs and money,' said Cardolp.

'Dr Cardolp, your opinions are as meaningless as they are welcome.' Dr Matlock was getting bored.

'Well it's true, isn't it? Why are they here otherwise?' he spluttered.

'Shut up Cardolp, you pathetic man.' Dr Matlock turned back to Bert. 'I think perhaps you need to be honest with your sister Mr Fairwold. It seems you haven't been telling her the truth.'

Bert became a different person before Polly's eyes; he took on the look of a mad man as the atmosphere got colder around him.

'She can either hear it from you or us. It's completely your choice,' continued Dr Matlock, her voice steady and unnerved. 'Your brother, Ms Fairwold, has chosen to put you at risk, you and everyone else. Seeing as he won't speak, perhaps I can explain to you what's been going on.' She paused to sip her coffee. 'Your brother has become involved with an organisation that's responsible for the deaths of many innocent people. They have a misguided belief that they are protecting the citizens of Overthere. Although that's not your reason, is it Mr Fairwold? Yours is a little less heroic than that. Your reason is simple: you are exacting revenge.'

'I don't believe you. Bert wouldn't hurt a fly, would you Bert.' It was a statement, not a question, but Bert refused to acknowledge Polly and instead kept his face fixed, as if in a trance and not part of the conversation.

Polly wondered if she knew the man sitting next to her, the man who had been missing for the last 10 years. When she thought about his reasons for his disappearance, they were weak against the backdrop of this new information. What had he told her about the attacks? Hadn't he hinted at something? She'd been so worried he would leave again that she hadn't scrutinised his story, she hadn't read between the lines or pushed him for more information. They had been playing, hadn't they? As they had as children.

'It seems very likely to us, Ms Fairwold, that your brother has been using you as his last line of protection.'

'I don't understand what you mean, he hasn't used me at all.' Polly choked back her tears.

'Really? Are you sure about that? Think Ms Fairwold, and this is serious, it's not a game. Why are you here otherwise? Did you decide to come here of your own accord?'

'It was completely my own choice,' protested Polly, though her mind was working ahead of her. Why was she here if not because of Bert? He was the reason Donald came to visit her. Ever since then she'd only had his information to go on. What was more likely – would her brother use her? If only he'd deny it. That was what was troubling her the most. Why wasn't he telling them how ridiculous this all was? Did he believe the Official Police were a threat?

'I can see you are sceptical, but I implore you now to think about what this man has told you. I assume he believes us to be attacking Overs and disposing of them.'

'Well you did take Donald, didn't you?' Polly said defiantly.

'We did bring Mr Pigeon in for questioning. I assure you he's perfectly safe. We brought him in to find your brother Ms Fairwold.' She sipped at her coffee again, elegantly placing it down on the table; she had such small, delicate hands. 'We may have used unorthodox methods to question him, but we couldn't be sure how involved Donald was himself. We knew Mr Fairwold was returning to the capital. You and Donald were the only connections we knew about. Your brother and his organisation have been planning an attack for some time. We took Donald as soon as he contacted you.'

'Bert, please say something,' Polly appealed to her brother. 'This isn't true, is it?'

She reached out to touch his cheek, looking for a connection, some form of reassurance that they'd got it wrong. He flinched away from her, slapping her hand away, shaking her off. She felt as if he'd kicked her. She was swallowing a raw form of poison, it slipped down inside her, sickening her, she felt utterly lost, not scared, something worse than that. It was a realisation of something she didn't want to acknowledge.

'It's not true,' she said again, this time without conviction.

'YES IT IS Ms Fairwold. And what's more, you know it is. The question now is, will you follow in your Brother's stupidity? Do you, too, believe an attack is necessary?'

'No, I don't want to hurt anybody. I don't even understand what is going on,' Polly answered, as honestly as she could.

'Good, I'm relieved to hear you say that. So, we need you to think now Ms Fairwold, if Mr Fairwold won't speak – do you still believe you're doing the right thing by protecting him?'

'You moron, you utter moron!' Bert erupted. Polly looked around, and his eyes told her all she needed to know. 'You don't get it, none of you do, they are going to destroy Overthere.' He was breathing heavily, his eyes blazed.

'Mr Fairwold, how could we possibly do that? We don't even know where it is. I understand your distrust in this organisation, and I concede that you are right when you believe the world is at risk. Many leaders around the globe desire the destruction of Overthere, but the vital point you are missing is that your anger is misguided. I correct myself, your anger is contributing to the destruction of this planet, but you are too vain and too stupid to see.'

'Vanity. I don't care about vanity. I don't care what happens to me.' A bit of spit ejected itself forcefully from Bert's mouth.

'That is precisely the flaw in your logic. You believe you are the one who has the answer. You believe only you and your crew understand what's happening and only you can solve it. That is where your vanity lies. The fact you can't see it makes you dangerous, dangerous to yourself.' Dr Matlock edged closer to Bert.

'Oh, are you trying to tell me I'm mad now? How typical. Can you hear this Polly? This is how they get you.' Bert turned to her grabbing at Polly's hands.

'No, not mad Mr Fairwold, ill-educated, misinformed and unaware. You have killed innocent people Mr Fairwold, what gives you that right?' Dr Matlock looked almost curious.

Luc Smith stepped forward and held Bert tightly by the arms.

'What gives *you* that right? The government has killed many innocent people, but because you have a name, because you do it as a business. What about all the needless wars?' Bert's body writhed with anger and at the restriction.

'The government is accountable and elected. I am not claiming all decisions made are the right ones. Again, I agree that we need to be more responsible, but this is not an upper-sixth-form argument, there are reasons and responsibilities that we have to take. Still, we're not talking about that. This is your vendetta, Mr Fairwold, and your ego. You have murdered men, woman and children.' The certainty of Dr Matlock's accusations made Polly feel very small.

Dr Matlock words sunk into her heart. Polly, who up until this point had hoped somehow there had been a big mistake, suddenly calmly accepted the situation. Although her heart shattered, it was at least a breakthrough.

Dr Matlock turned to her as if sensing it. 'You do have a choice Ms Fairwold. You and Donald may walk away now, leaving Bert in our custody, or you can fight a public battle.

You will be the one that suffers the most, as the things your brother has done will not please you.'

'I'd like to see Donald,' she replied, turning away from the strange man she'd walked in the room with, and had once known as her brother.

Chapter 14. Madagascar

'What do you think you're doing?' Dr Matlock appeared from nowhere in her room. Polly was sniffing at a bottle of something called Royal Jelly, trying to identify its intended purpose. It certainly wasn't edible, she'd learned to her dismay.

'Oh um, I'm running a bath,' answered Polly, gesturing to the bathroom door where she was indeed running a bath.

For a brief moment, Polly thought Dr Matlock might spontaneously combust, as her lips tightened and a small vein in her temple began visibly pulsating.

'This isn't a hotel, you're not on holiday,' she snapped.

'I'm sorry,' said Polly, not sure what she was apologising for. Perhaps she was late for breakfast. 'What time is breakfast?' she enquired.

'You have fifteen minutes until we resume questioning.' Dr Matlock stalked out.

Polly's unfathomable guilt made her cross. Why put her in a room with a bath if she *wasn't* supposed to use it?

She sank into the soothing hot water. Her mind let go of all the whizzing thoughts. Minutes passed, as she watched the bubbles rise and fall over her tummy. Logically, now her thoughts over the last few days began to reorder themselves. First, meeting Donald and him arriving on her doorstep. She played out the scene in her head trying to remember what she'd said and what he'd said. She was alarmed to find herself altering her memories to invite him inside instead. On reflection, he took on a new, different quality. She found it exciting thinking about him. Her mind wandered on into the fantasy. He was leaning towards her, telling her that she was beautiful, when she was suddenly jolted from her thoughts by scalding her big toe on the hot tap. Bert lurched his ugly head into her thoughts. He'd turned up out of the blue. She knew something wasn't right. Why had he come back after all this time? He'd not explained himself at all. It was frustrating that she hadn't asked him directly; they'd had time, lots of chances, but she hadn't. She thought back to him talking about Janet and the house he'd taken her to in Stockwell. It suddenly dawned on her that that flat didn't seem to belong to him. Now she realised, it looked ransacked and those books were not his books. They had stayed in someone else's house; of that she was sure.

The creeping sickness stole over her again as she remembered Dr Matlock's words – 'He has killed innocent people' and 'He is leading a crusade'. What had he done? Try as hard as she could, Polly couldn't associate these actions with the Bert she knew; the one who had put a washing up bowl on his head as a kid, the one who drew her a picture of a spaceship for her sixth birthday. She separated the two Berts, good Bert and evil Bert. That made it easier; a childlike notion to explain away the murders.

Polly was no longer a child.

Somewhere along the way, Bert had committed awful crimes and was seemingly hellbent to commit more. Polly had always been the one to play the stupid role, the one who forgot everything and was silly. He'd taken that away from her now. Bert was the thinker, the educator, the traveller. She recalled the look on his face just 12 hours ago. Smug, that was it, he was proud of himself and thought he was so clever. Polly sat up and splashed water over herself.

Dressed and anxious, Polly stood to wait with Mr Luc Smith. He didn't make any attempt to engage with her. Robotic in his actions, he escorted her into a windowless, small, diamond-shaped room. Dr Matlock and Mr Cardolp entered, without Bert this time. They looked serious, in the way balloons aren't.

Answering the same questions from the day before, she explained Donald arriving at her door. The code she was given, trying to find him, Tony the taxi driver's help, Bert turning up, going to the pub, the ransacked house, the tv appeal, everything.

    'And is there anything at all that you can think of that might have happened, or something extraordinary?' asked Mr Cardolp again.

    'Aside from an alien turning up at my house? Giving me a secret code and disappearing? Has anything else extraordinary happened?' asked Polly sarcastically.

All this was lost on Andreas Cardolp, who wasn't big on sarcasm. 'Yes, can you remember anything else?' he repeated.

'Can I get anyone a drink?' A young, keen looking man popped his head around the door.

'Get out.' Dr Matlock's voice was ice. She didn't shout, she almost hissed.

Cardolp's heart filled with glee. 'Simon, you were under strict instructions not to enter this room. We will have words,' he said, barely able to contain his delight in the young man's error.

'Oh sorry. It's just when you said to "pop in now" and then to see if we need anything, I thought that's what you wanted me to do. My apologies for the misunderstanding,' said Simon, light-heartedly beaming at them all with a lovely smile.

Dr Matlock's eyes flickered over to Cardolp, who was silently and brutally murdering the young officer in his mind.

Not taking her eyes of Cardolp, she changed tone. 'Coffee for me Simon, black, please. Ms Fairwold?'

'I would love a cup of tea,' Polly beamed back at Simon, grateful for a reprieve.

'Do you take milk?' he asked.

'Yes please.' Who the hell drinks black tea? She thought inwardly. This Simon kid was not a full set of picnic sandwiches after all.

'Ah that's a shame, we're out of milk. I could go and get some?' Polly wasn't sure how to answer that question.

'Tea with milk Simon. Go now.' Dr Matlock turned her back on the lad, who nodded and pottered off whistling to himself.

A familiar jingle took over Polly. It was at least a minute before she realised it wasn't a jingle, but a memory rising to the top of her brain.

'Madagascar,' she said out loud.

It was the first time that Dr Matlock looked genuinely puzzled.

'The garage! I've just remembered. It's probably not important at all, but something odd did happen, shortly after Bert turned up. I'd run out of milk – no, actually that's not true, I never have milk because I always forget to buy it and'

'Polly,' it was the first time Dr Matlock had used her first name when addressing her, 'please get on with it. I don't need to know why you don't have milk.'

'Righty ho. So yes, as I was saying, I needed to get milk and went out to get some. There's this garage near my house, well at least I think it might be a garage, and it's got a neon sign outside saying Madagascar. When I was walking back, there was a strange man with a big red beard'

She stopped talking, as both Dr Matlock, Cardolp and Luc Smith all seemed to be staring at her intently.

'Go on please Polly. Did you speak to him?' Dr Matlock asked levelly.

'Yes, I did. I said something and he said nothing.'

'He stopped talking to you?' Cardolp paused momentarily from furiously taking notes.

'No, he said "nothing". Those were the words he used. I think he then said something like "We didn't expect you" or "We weren't expecting you so soon."' Polly tried hard to remember his exact words.

'What did you do?' Cardolp asked.

'Oh, I ran away. It seemed the bravest thing to do,' said Polly.

'Can you explain to us exactly what this man looked like?' Dr Matlock asked.

'I think so, but it was pretty brief. He was very tall, with a massive, red beard and a bald head. I think that made his beard look bigger. It was enormous.' Polly was trying to demonstrate the size of the beard with her hands.

'That's him. I'll pick him up,' said Luc Smith, getting up without hesitation.

'Yes, but be careful Smith. I don't want you, or him, to end up dead,' Dr Matlock instructed, momentarily forgetting Polly was still in the room. Her eyes met Polly to see if the comment had registered.

'That's who? Who's him?' It was Polly's turn to look confused.

All three of them ignored her, picked up their things and left Polly in the room. The door opened a minute later, but it was only Simon with her tea. All attempts to get information from him were useless. He did, however, give her a good update on the milk situation.

He left her miserably sniffing at her black tea with a lemony hint.

Chapter 15. Donald's secret mission

In the spirit of 'a problem shared is a problem doubled', we won't go into the details of the next few hours of Polly's life. Polly wished her room freshly painted, as watching it dry would have given her endless joy in comparison.

Alone with her thoughts, they eventually brought her back to Donald Pigeon. She wondered for the thousandth time why he had given her that code. Did it mean anything?

Had Donald thought about her at all these past days? Maybe she was only another bit of background fodder in his epic universe. To someone born on another planet, someone like her must seem reasonably insignificant. Building a list of questions to ask him in her head had become her daily occupation. What was Overthere like? Was it similar to Earth? She'd heard somewhere that it had a sea and that it was purple. How old was he? When had he left Overthere? Her questions lead to more questions. What was he here for? Did they share the same emotions? Did he have feelings? Was he a *he* at all? Did that even matter?

Like a dog trying to catch its tail, her mind went round and round.

She got up and paced around the small room, playing out different scenarios for when they next met. She'd think of something very amusing to say, she'd work out what that was later. Donald would see her and say something like

'Wow you're so funny' and then she'd say something brilliant. He says 'You're so smart, I have travelled across the universe and never found anyone as smart and funny' then he would add 'and beautiful' under his breath. She would say 'What did you say?' and she would look at him and then...

'Ouch!' Her thoughts were thwarted by the door abruptly introducing itself to her head.

'Are you OK?' At the top of a long pair of legs, the star of her imagination stood over her.

It was only the second time meeting him, but she felt overjoyed at such a friendly face.

Donald seemed taller than before and not as thin. Having only seen him once, Polly had started to think she might not remember what he looked like, but her memory snapped into place.

He frowned a little. 'Are you OK? You're not hurt, are you?'

Polly looked at him dumbly and laughed. It was a strange laugh that went a little high in the middle. 'Oh I'm fine. What are you doing here?' Her head hurt.

'Good question, I'm not sure. They've just brought me here,' Donald said, smiling at her.

Suddenly an urge took over Polly and she threw her arms around him. 'I'm so pleased you're OK,' she said. Then thought how strange it was that he didn't feel remotely alien, he felt incredibly familiar. Stepping back from him, embarrassed. Donald beamed back at her and her embarrassment melted away.

'I was picked up when I left your house the other day. I'm not sure what it is that's happening, but they are looking for your brother, Bert,' said Donald.

'They have him,' Polly said. 'He turned up the day after you arrived. We've been trying to find you. What has he done? Do you know?'

'No idea, I...' he faltered. 'I suppose you know that I'm not – um what's the right way to say this? – I was not born on Earth.'

'I know,' interrupted Polly, to save him from struggling. 'Well, I guessed. Is that why they arrested you?' she said, suddenly angry on his behalf in case this was true.

'I thought so at first, but they seemed more interested in Bert. I was expecting my arrest and felt sure they were going to lock me up for good, or worse. But, then I was brought to see you.' He looked thoughtful. 'I suppose they can't think me a threat if they've let me come and speak to you. And what about you, have they mistreated you? Did they arrest you too?'

Polly did her best to explain the last few days. She left out a few pieces of information, such as broadcasting to the world that she and Donald were married. It seemed a minor part of the overall story that needed more time to explain adequately.

While talking, she'd taken hold of his hand; he hadn't seemed to notice. Becoming aware of their skin touching made her feel funny again; perhaps she hit her head harder than she thought.

'Ah, look at the two love birds.' Simon, the policeman, came barging in through the door of the tiny octagonal room. Polly went to let go of Donald's hand, blushing shamefully, but he wouldn't let go and held on tight.

'You're both getting on well then. Good, good.' Simon continued in his merry way, popping down a massive stack of files on the table. Donald and Polly exchanged a look to check if the other understood what was going on and quickly established neither of them had a clue.

'Just a few forms to fill in, then you can both be on your way,' Simon said, taking out a pen from his little tin pencil case that had red trucks on it.

'Are you sure?' said Polly. 'I was pretty certain that we were still needed. What about Bert?' she asked as an afterthought.

'Can't tell you anything I'm afraid. I need you to sign these forms and then you can go home. I bet you're both looking forward to getting home, hey?' He grinned with an exaggerated wink. Simon, Polly decided quickly, was a nosey twit.

Polly stopped asking questions after that. She did want to get out of this place; better to get out first and ask questions later – that was to be her adopted motto.

Several hours later, and with hands covered in black ink, they found themselves outside 49 Farringdon Road. The dusty, noisy metropolis roared by while our two, seemingly disinterested, adventurers stood in the street shadows awaiting a cab. Donald was the first to speak. 'Would it be OK if I came to your house? There's so much to talk about,' he stammered.

'Of course.' Polly assumed that was happening anyway. Inwardly she cringed. Why am I so embarrassed? I do not understand what is happening to me, make it stop, make it stop, she silently lamented. An inward, and rather harsh voice that sounded a bit like her mother, gave her a stern talking to – 'Come on, what are you playing at, cut this nonsense out. It's no time to mess around with aliens, you're supposed to be a grown-up.'

They arrived back in Putney just as the environmental disposal experts, or 'bin men' as Polly still called them, were trying their best to pick out little bits of plastic from the rubbish and discard it willy-nilly across the street. They walked around to Polly's flat.

'What?' Polly glared at Donald. Donald, for his part, was looking at a single piece of glass on the pavement.

'Oh, so don't even bother talking then,' Polly continued. Somewhere between the cab and the door,

Polly had got herself worked up into a roaring rage with Donald Pigeon. She had no idea why this change of heart had occurred, although someone a little wiser may have put it down to vulnerability.

'What? Sorry, I mean, *pardon*? Do you know this path is littered with glass? It's everywhere. I didn't even notice the first time I was here, this is a health hazard.' It was if he was talking to himself.

'Is that the only thing you are interested in?' replied Polly, in a voice more huffily than intended. 'As if that was the most important thing on Earth or...Overthere...no, no, no!' Polly so rudely interrupted by Donald collecting shards of glass from her path.

'You are unbearable and a weirdo. Can we please go inside?' Polly blurted this out and then, seeing the look on Donald's face, felt as if she'd just torn off every petal from the most delicate of flowers. Donald's eyes linked with hers and she suddenly realised that she'd embarrassed him.

'Oh, I just thought it would be safer if I picked up the glass. You may cut your feet, or, well, it was silly of me I suppose.' He looked at her as if hoping for her forgiveness.

The concern, the gesture and his awkwardness made her heart hurt so much that she wanted to swoop all six foot of him up in her arms and tell him she loved him.

'Yeah great, well done, let's go in,' Polly replied, in what she hoped was a jokey, light sort of tone.

Polly went straight to the bathroom when they got in. She gave herself a long look in the mirror. Am I attractive to him? She wondered, staring at her face, taking in her dark, frizzy hair, her glasses, the shine on her nose; she could only see where improvements could be. She thought about her previous relationships. Did it even matter how she looked? A fat, wet tear fell down her face. The voice returned. 'Stop it, this is stupid, who cares what anyone thinks about your looks, you're OK, stop making up love stories.' Belittled, she hastily washed her hand and returned to the living room. Donald was still hovering at the top of the stairs.

'You can sit down,' she said, trying to make her voice sound neutral.

Donald made for one of the kitchen chairs. She noticed he was limping a bit.

'You are allowed to sit on the sofa,' she said, getting annoyed again by his timidity.

'Oh, sorry, I...well, Bert said not to sit on the most comfortable seats, it's rude,' he said, while hobbling towards the sofa.

'Bert's a twit,' Polly replied, turning her back on Donald and filling up the kettle noisily. She wondered what the devil was up with her today; was she becoming neurotic?

Donald paused and looked at her, unsure what to do. 'Do you hate him?' he asked, moving towards the kitchen chairs again.

'Will you please, please, sit down. No, not on the kitchen chair, on the sofa,' she almost shouted. Naturally, he obeyed and she watched him wince as he eased himself onto the sofa. Anger swelled inside her once again.

'What did the Official Police do to you, did they beat you up?' A pang of guilt hit her. She'd left Bert with those people.

'What are you talking about? Oh no, I see.' He sussed out she was referring to his limping and wincing. 'It's not what you think. It's a little embarrassing. I fell down the stairs on my way to see you this afternoon,' Donald confessed.

Polly looked sceptical. 'No, really, I was rushing and I'm still not used to your level of gravity and well...' Donald petered out.

Polly could see the sunshine once more and let out a little laugh. 'Oh, well don't worry. I fall over all the time and I'm used to the gravity,' said Polly, settling things. 'What do we do now?'

'You didn't answer my question – do you hate Bert? Overians can't hate, therefore I'm curious to know what it would take,' said Donald.

Polly thought about it. 'I suppose I should. If he has hurt innocent people. I certainly hate that he did that.' She let out a sigh. 'But hate him? No, I don't think I do, as stupid and dangerous as he was, I can't bring myself to hate him.'

'That's good, really good. I am experiencing guilt. I think that a lot of this is the fault of Overians, and mine by extension,' admitted Donald.

'Why?' asked Polly.

'Well, it goes like this – if Overians weren't so fascinated by earthlings and the need to intervene in their impending demise, then I would not have been sent here with Janet. Had I not come here, Bert would not have met me. If Bert hadn't met me, he wouldn't have met Janet. Janet was a friend, you see – we were part of the same envoy. Janet and I were both quite radical and idealistic when we first came here. We naively thought we were helping Earth. We thought we were doing a good thing by introducing ourselves and coming to help. I can see how we were well-intentioned, but ignorant of how people on Earth lived.' He paused briefly to sip his tea.

'I'm a bit lost,' admitted Polly.

'I'm so sorry, it's such a lot for you to understand. I don't want to upset you.' He looked at her quickly, as if trying to pass something meaningful across, before diverting his eyes to stare at the wall behind her. It was as if they were having a conversation on three different levels: words, energy and actions had contradicted one another, until Polly was left overwhelmed and in the dark.

'That bit you said about Earth's impending demise is a bit concerning,' levelled Polly. 'What exactly is going to happen?' she asked.

He remained silent.

'Please,' she looked down at her shoes, 'there's so much I want to know. I'm not even sure what the right questions are to ask you. Please don't worry about upsetting me. I get upset over advertisements with dogs frolicking around with toilet roll. It doesn't matter if you talk or not.'

'Don't panic. I'll tell you everything you want to know,' reassured Donald.

For the first time in her life, Polly really and truly listened. It felt very odd at first to hear him talk about Earth the same way someone might speak of a far-off land. Very quickly, the oddness manifested into fascination. It wasn't solely the talk of intergalactic travel, space, time and the universe; Donald fascinated her. He could be reading the contents of a custard mix and she'd be listening.

'Tell me first about Bert,' she said decidedly. 'What happened between him and Janet and who did he hurt? How was he using me? Was that why he came back? How did you meet?'

'OK, OK, one question at a time. Bert and I met through work, and we got chatting. We'd go for the odd drink after work and moan about Gary – that was our boss.' He looked a little guilty.

'I know, I met him,' agreed Polly.

'Did you? I'm sorry you had to go through that,' said Donald sincerely.

'It's OK. I've met worse,' Polly confirmed.

'Really? I don't envy you that. Anyway, where was I? Yes, we'd go for the odd pint, we weren't that close, and then one night, Janet turned up at the pub. She had been living in the US but travelled to the UK and was out with work colleagues.'

'And you and she were both envoys from Overthere?' interjected Polly.

'Yes. All envoys are assessed and trained by country and then grouped according to Earth alliances. It makes it easier to integrate. Janet was selected for the US, so I was more than a little surprised to see her. The last time I'd seen her was on Overthere,' Donald continued.

'How did you get here?' asked Polly.

'That's jumping the gun a bit. We teleported, obviously – I'll explain that later. Bert and Janet met that night and fell in love, I suppose.' Donald looked queerly at Polly as he said this.

'And she died, right?' added Polly, keen to get to the teleportation bit.

'No,' he said.

'What? Wait, but Bert said she died. Was he lying?' asked Polly. Now she was confused again; it didn't take a lot.

'I think he does genuinely believe that something has happened to her and that she is dead. But no, she left him. And, for the record, we don't die,' Donald levelled.

'Then why does he still claim she's dead?' Polly paused for a second before the last bit of information hit. 'You don't die?'

'Hmm, well yes, it was a worrying development at the time. I think it made it easier for him to blame someone else or something else for her leaving. It backed up his deluded conspiracies.' He paused. 'And no, we don't die on Overthere.'

'The conspiracies are not a new thing? But he was so convincing.' Polly couldn't yet absorb what *not dying* could mean. It was like showing a mouse the theory of relativity; it did not compute.

'He's convincing because he believes them to be true. His sense of reason and logic has left him. He can't turn back, because that would mean having to face all his mistakes and accept responsibility.' Donald gave Polly a meaningful look.

'What has happened to Janet? Where is she? Has she returned to Overthere?' Polly picked at her teacup.

'Oh goodness no, she's alive and living in Bromley.'

'Bromley? Where on earth is that?' Polly puzzled.

'No idea.' Donald shrugged.

'So, who did Bert hurt? Did you know about it?' She pushed herself to ask these questions but, in truth, didn't want to know the answers.

'I knew that he was unbalanced, but it was only last week when I realised how serious things had got. I believe the attack at Barons Court was him.'

'But that killed 13 people,' gasped Polly.

Donald said nothing and stopped himself. There was something else he felt guilty about, but Polly had suddenly figured it out.

'Ah, you told him about the code so that he'd get in touch with me,' she said.

'I never thought in a million years he'd try and use you for his protection. Honestly, I had no idea. I'm so sorry, I just thought that, if he got back in touch with you, he might return to some rational thought. He talked of you so often. I thought I was getting him help, but instead, I endangered you.'

He looked as if he might cry. Polly put her arms around him. 'Stop taking the blame. It's not your fault.'

He didn't look remotely comforted and looked down at Polly. She couldn't quite understand the look. She suddenly felt an act of great courage that she'd never felt before. Lifting herself on the tips of her toes, she kissed him.

There was a nanosecond in time where it felt like the world could have taken two very different paths. In a nanosecond, every type of emotion rushed through Polly's body. It felt that she might implode and then, just as soon as she became remotely aware, it disappeared. A warm, liquid silky feeling flooded through her as Donald reciprocated pressure against her lips.

Her brain shifted to a higher realm, leaving her with a distinct understanding of everything. At this moment she could explain it all – she could have made a T-shirt that always showed the front no matter which way you looked at it, completed an eight-dart finish or scored a hattrick with one shot at goal. It was a glance, a glint of sparkles and gold, a spec of the most vivid and beautiful colour she'd ever seen.

The beautiful moment evaporated as her lips left him and she became aware that he had withdrawn. A creeping sense of loss and despair crawled under her fingernails and beneath her scalp.

Donald looked back at her and smiled.

'An earthling's brain is probably the most complex thing to an earthling. But to an observer from another planet, it is a very cute, yet simple, thing.' He flipped her nose with his finger.

'Like a radio,' he ventured. 'The brain is one collected consciousness, a sort of broadcast of thoughts. There are billions and trillions of thoughts occurring every second, every nanosecond.' Donald seemed unstoppable now. Polly allowed him to continue his strange chatter. 'Each brain has its radio and each radio is different. But the radio itself is not generating the content or thoughts, the thoughts are broadcast from multiple locations. No individual earthling has control over the broadcast and yet it belongs to everyone. It's a beautiful design.'

'Thank you?' Polly wasn't sure if it was a compliment or not.

'Earthling brains also have another function, which is rooted in the physical world.' He took a sip of tea and calmly carried on. 'There are two potential viruses that can attack – one is a psychosis, known to occur when a paradox is present, the other is a negative feedback loop, where a new thought is copied and repeated over and over, much to the discomfort of the earthling. These viruses are incredibly useful for many things that Overthere has developed. Using these so-called *viruses* we figured out how to teleport through space, prevent death and live in harmony.' Donald stretched out his body and seemed to relax.

'Can we do that too? Can earthlings teleport through space?' Polly asked in wide-eyed astonishment.

'An earthling is currently unable to physically and mentally transport itself from one area of space because:

1. They have created a governance called 'time' that prevents them from imagining they can.
2. They are unable to connect to their collective consciousness and don't yet understand their collective abilities.
3. They wouldn't know where to go, because they don't believe anywhere else other than Earth exists. Tricky to get somewhere you don't think is there.
4. There isn't a four, but I like even numbers,' Donald joked.

Polly's brain felt like a smudge of glue and her stomach as if she'd swallowed a glob of larvae.

'We're idiots?' she said, trying to find something comfortable to cling to. Wondering when might be the time to bring up the fact she'd kissed him, and he'd not mentioned it.

'No, far from it, you're just very new in universal terms,' said Donald enthusiastically. 'In many respects you are fascinating and brilliant.' Polly blushed, until she realised he was referring to her as an earthling, not as an individual.

'OK, so assuming we figure out one and two before the sun dies...where is Overthere?' Polly asked, feeling very grown-up all of a sudden. She was talking to an alien about space travel, for real.

'Overthere is only three-thousand galaxies away, about 20-billion miles or so,' answered Donald.

'If I could get you in a headlock, I could show you, but I'm afraid I might blow your mind.'

'Don't flatter yourself,' said Polly gruffly, still annoyed he'd not mentioned the kiss.

'I wasn't. The odds of me blowing your mind are 98-to-1,' said Donald, as he gently pulled her closer to him.

Chapter 16: The lost night

It was the longest and shortest night Polly had ever observed. They talked and talked, shared music, shared thoughts and looked at the Moon. Polly explained why it was so beautiful to an enthused Donald.

It was 8 am when she told Donald that she'd fallen in love with him.

Polly didn't quite get the reaction she was expecting; Donald said thank you and then fell into a form of meditation. It was as if a grey-blue mist had formed around him. Polly felt crushed and elated at the same time.

Polly felt too alive to let this meditation become transcendental; it was something about the shape of his face that she wanted to make him aware of. As he stirred back into the same realm, bliss turned to horror.

A bashing sound at the door shattered any sense of peace they had built between them.

Polly felt sick again as she opened the door to four heavy-looking men.

'Are you Polly Fairwold?' said one heavy.

'Umm, yes...sorry, but how did you get past the front door?' she asked.

'We have the keys,' another bruiser piped up.

'Why didn't you let yourself in then?' Polly asked sarcastically.

'We didn't want to disrespect your privacy,' they said in unison.

'How incredibly conscientious of you,' Polly quipped, the sarcasm utterly lost to the ether.

'My name is PC Dave. We have reason to believe you are holding a suspect on your premises. May we come in?' PC Dave poked his head through the door and peered around.

Polly hoped that Donald had had the foresight to jump out of the window, but remembered they were legally released.

'He's not done anything wrong, and he's not under a...what did you call it?...' Polly struggled to find the words.

'...warrant,' answered Donald, appearing behind her.

'It's not our job to ask questions,' responded PC Dave.

'You said that wrong Dave,' another heavy with a squeaky voice butted in unexpectedly.

'Shut up Keith. I know what I said, and I mean it. We have a warrant to search these premises. Before we infringe on your premises, you should know, if you don't say now, this will be held against you in court,' Dave continued.

'I don't have a clue what this is about.' Polly was starting to feel annoyed.

'Do you know where we can find Mr Bert Fairwold and does he reside in this property?' Dave asked.

'No. You already have Bert, don't you? Don't tell me you imbeciles have lost him?' Polly felt brave with Donald cowering behind her.

'Are you Mr Fairwold?' said Dave, eying Donald.

'No, I am not,' answered Donald in earnest.

'You have him! Dr Matlock has him, you know, Dr Matlock from the special division of the police. Are you the police?' Polly had given up being polite.

All five heavies – one having just materialised, as if from nowhere – instantly displayed their intricately detailed police badges to prove who they were.

'I told you, didn't I?' Keith continued, poking the lead police officer in the shoulder. 'It was a stupid idea to prioritise our emergency response calls reverse alphabetically.'

'How was I to know that Bert Fairwold would turn out to be the most important?' Dave turned on Keith.

'Because they told us he was the most important one to catch three days ago.' Keith looked smug.

'But they say that about everyone. Look, I'm not going through this again, we agreed this was the system, and besides, no one had any better ideas.' Dave looked set to explode. 'So, you're not hiding him then?' He turned back to Polly.

'No, he's been caught. Well, not caught, we brought him to Dr Matlock two days ago,' Polly confirmed.

Polly noticed two of the police officers, who hadn't said anything, walking away down the corridor. She could have sworn one of them muttered 'morons' as they left earshot.

'Well in which case, we're sorry for wasting your time. But next time, don't withhold information from us,' said Dave firmly.

'But we didn't.' Polly was utterly confused now.

'You talk nonsense,' squeaked Keith.

'Shut up Keith.' Dave lost it.

Exasperated and amused, Polly shut the door on the quarrel and turned back to face Donald.

'Do you think he might have escaped?' Donald asked.

'I'd say it's unlikely, but we probably should check. I don't want to deal with that lot again.' Donald peered through the spy hole on the door.

'I suppose you're right,' sighed Polly. 'I'll get us a cab.' She picked up her phone and felt scared. The whole world had changed. One minute she was elated, the next on the floor.

Life was a lot easier when she wasn't chasing terrorists, trying to figure out her dreams and kissing aliens.

Chapter 17. Bye-bye Bert

> Love is something if you give you away, give it away, give it away,
> Love is something if you give it away, you'll end up having more,
> It's just like a magic penny, hold it tight and you won't have any, but lend it, spend it and you'll have so many, they'll roll all over the floor for,
> Love is something, if you give it away, you'll end up having more.
>
> Malvina Reynolds, 'Magic Penny', 1958.

'I don't care what you have to do but make that man shut up.' An angry-looking Dr Andres Cardolp stalked into the room where Donald and Polly sat waiting to see Bert Fairwold.

In a room back at 49 Farringdon road, an exhausted-looking Bert met Polly's eyes as he sat down in front of her.

At first, he didn't seem to recognise her. His eyes were unfocused and his presence a shock to Polly. She'd expected him to have escaped but, now she saw him, she suddenly didn't want to be there anymore. Why was she here?

'Polly,' he said at last, as he seemed to enter back into the world, 'where have you been? What is going on?

Can you tell them I didn't mean to do it? It was Janet's fault.'

'What on earth did happen with you and Janet? I want to know the truth,' demanded Polly.

'She's gone, it doesn't matter. Can you help me, Polly?' Bert pleaded.

Answer me you goddamn looney, screamed Polly's inner voice, but outwardly she said, 'How can you expect me to do anything? What could *I* do to help *you*?'

'Tell them I am innocent. Tell them to...please Polly.'

'Are you innocent?' she asked.

'Please tell them I am innocent, I need, I want, I need' he trailed off and went back into his world, humming away to himself.

Polly's head swam. It was upsetting. She'd only come to see if he was OK and now she was torn. Was she supposed to look after him?

So many people have written such beautiful things about love. In Polly's small world, love had been difficult to come across and, despite his 10-year absence, Polly had loved her brother. Even now, she could empathise with him. Not that she could forgive what he'd done, but she still loved him. Thinking of that was unbearable, but she didn't believe in good people and bad people; that would have made her decision easier, if she did.

Polly could suddenly see before her a parallel life. The one where she would look after Bert, visit him regularly, fight his corner. Her future – she could see very clearly – wouldn't be unhappy. Here was where the blinding realisation kicked in. He wasn't a version of Bert she had ever known. He had chosen to become this person, and she no longer recognised him. It was a relief. Her happiness was not along this path. Her certainty made her want to walk out immediately.

Despite this feeling, she listened to him prattle on, knowing that this would be the last time she saw him, and a few minutes wouldn't make any difference.

'I can't remember what she looks like anymore,' wailed Bert.

Polly looked at him, shaken by the manic look in his eye.

'I speak to her over and over in my head. She used to be clear, and now she is distant. She no longer tells me what I need to know.' He sobbed deeply.

'What do you need to know?' asked Polly, trying to remain calm.

'I need to know what to do. I need to know how to make everything alright. I love her. Where is she?' Bert whimpered.

'I don't know,' said Polly sadly.

He looked at her suddenly with wild eyes. 'Get out and leave me alone!' he screamed, leaping up and scratching at her arms.

Polly had seen enough. She didn't need to know anything more and scuttled out of the room without looking back.

'Come to me my darling. Tell me, sweetheart, tell me everything's OK. Sing me the song, sing me to sleep, sing me to sleep.' Bert's trembling voice followed her down the corridor.

Chapter 18. Bye-bye Donald

'The code was made up?' A cold, blank Polly stared unblinkingly at Donald, willing some kind of connection between them that wasn't forthcoming. 'It was a way to get to Bert, wasn't it?' She felt deflated. 'If you convinced Bert that you had the code, he might try to use it to get Janet back.' Polly sipped her tea and wondered how long this moment might last.

'Oh, no, that's not right. The code is as real as you or I. I still have to leave Earth though,' said Donald.

'Really?' said Polly, sitting up sharply. 'Why won't you stay then? Explain it to me,' she demanded.

'I can't tell you I'm afraid.' Donald shrugged his shoulders, leaned over and pulled at her frizzy hair. He had a habit of doing it. She liked it.

'Why won't you tell me?' She looked at him from under her eyelashes, hoping she was coming across as adorable and cursing herself for it.

'It's not that I won't, it's that I can't.' He started playing with her hair.

'I don't quite understand,' said Polly, distracted. She pushed his hands away.

'No. It doesn't make a great deal of sense.' Donald searched himself for a better way to explain. Eventually, he said, 'Think of it like this – imagine the start of something, the start of anything.'

'What, like a game? The start of a game?' said Polly, eying up a dusty box with 'Scrabble' written on it.

'Yes, that's a good example.' He nodded. 'Tell me how that game starts?'

'Well, you have a board and letters. You have to set up the board, there are these plastic trays, and you have to pick out seven letter tiles.' Polly's memories of playing endless games with her mum and dad made her yearn for them and lament her loss.

'Yes, you've got it,' interrupted Donald. 'Now let me ask you, is that the beginning of the game? The very beginning?'

'Yes...well, no...you need to have players first I guess.' Polly hoped this was going somewhere.

'Is that the beginning then? Finding players? Is that how Scrabble starts?' he pressed on, presumably going somewhere.

'Well yes, I think so. You'd also need to buy the game before you could play it,' she ventured.

'Good, good. So, try to imagine the start of Scrabble, where nothing else comes before it.'

'Before the players and getting the game?' asked Polly.

'Yes'

A silence reigned.

'I don't get it,' Polly confessed. 'Before the players and getting the game, someone would have to had to create the game.' She scrunched up her face a bit. This was like trying to understand infinity.

'And how did *they* create the game?' Donald pushed on, oblivious.

'I suppose *they* would have had to make it up in their heads. How does anyone make something up? I don't know. I wonder, who did create scrabble? I'm going to look it up...'

'No, no, Polly, come back here. You're going to have to concentrate now.' Donald looked at her intensely. 'How does anyone make something up?'

Polly's head hurt. 'Is this about God?'

'Maybe.' Donald shrugged his shoulders.

'I can't explain to you how it works. It is a code and it can give you anything you want, but I can't tell you how it works, because only *you* know how it works, as only *you* know what *you* want and only *you* know how to make it happen.' He sat back, looking pleased with himself.

After a pause, that could have been five minutes or 3,000 years, Polly thought she might have a vague idea what he was on about. But as soon as she'd caught a glimpse, it was gone again.

'It's often easier to think about what you want instead and work backwards,' confessed Donald.

'I have already made a list.' She scrambled around in her bag and dug out the envelope with her list of little big secret things, discovering on route a book she'd forgotten about. 'See, they are a bit stupid,' she said, handing over the list.

'No, they are not.' He looked over the list intently. 'What's a fountain pen?' asked Donald, momentarily distracted.

'Oh, it's a pen that you have to put an ink cartridge in. Don't know why it's called a fountain pen, maybe because it works as a fountain would...hang on I'll look it up.' She made for her phone again.

'No, don't worry, it doesn't matter,' he said, looking thoughtfully at the list.

'I could add to that list "finding out my purpose" if I even have one.' Polly stroked her chin.

'Do you think you do?' Donald asked.

'Well, funny you should ask that, because I never really thought I did, but when I was a kid, I used to think I was a fairy. A fairy that was here to clear up all of God's mistakes. I used to look at the clouds to tell me what to do, and I had all these friends that would help me out.' Suddenly she felt vulnerable. 'I know it sounds stupid, and I don't even know if I believe in God anyway. After my parents died and Bert left, I guess probably not. So, I had no purpose.' She ended abruptly to stop herself from bursting into tears.

'Does it matter if you have one or not?' he asked evenly.

'I don't know,' she answered truthfully.

'OK, well put it this way – let's say it didn't matter, then is there any harm in having one anyway and then setting out trying to achieve it?' He gave her a little nudge.

'I guess not. But what if it wasn't my purpose?' Polly put out her hand and Donald held on to it. His skin felt lovely.

'Well then, you would have at least worked out that, a) you have a purpose and, b) you could change what you were doing once you figured out what it was,' he said.

She couldn't fault his logic. 'Wait, what if I couldn't work out what it was?'

'You mean, what if you couldn't work out your purpose that doesn't exist?' He gave her a look.

'I guess it wouldn't matter because it wouldn't exist. So, I may as well try and find out. If I aim for getting what I want, then, if nothing else, I'll end up with what I want.' It all seemed so easy when she thought about it.

'Do you still want a boyfriend?' he asked her.

Polly looked up sharply. Was he messing her around? No, he looked, well, he looked the same as ever – like an adorable, friendly, tall, alien. He leaned towards her, pulling at her coat to draw her into him.

'Do you think you could date an alien?' he said. Her tummy did a backflip.

'Maybe,' she said, taking his hands. He bent down and gently kissed her. It was as if all the gods had come down to Earth to play their best songs.

'Where did you get that?' He pulled back from her, pointing in her handbag.

'What?' Polly asked.

'That book?' He was more excited than she'd ever seen him.

'Oh, this?' Polly held up the book called *Mentor Tome*. 'I found it at Bert's. It looked interesting. I sort of, um, borrowed it.'

'Oh, thank you, thank you, thank you. You are the most wonderful thing. I thought I'd lost it. Now I can get back.' He hopped in the air with glee.

'What do you mean "get back"?' she said, jumping back as though she'd stood on a mousetrap.

'Yes, this is what I was trying to tell you earlier, I have been recalled to Overthere. We all have. I'm one of the last ones left. Now I can go home.' He smiled so widely.

Polly wanted to run away, but her body wouldn't obey her mind, as she watched Donald turn the pages of the *Mentor Tome* in delight. It was like he'd always been there, even though she'd known him for, how long now? A few days, or a lifetime? No, no, no, he couldn't just leave now; he'd only just arrived!

'I'll come with you,' she announced.

He looked at her, as if only just realising what they both already knew. The look on his face told her everything.

'You can't,' he said, looking at the floor.

'WHY NOT?' Polly bellowed up into the air, at no one in particular; at a god, perhaps.

Chapter 19. The Mentor Tome

Mentor Tome – an extract

Translated into English in 1994 by Janet Planet.
Available in 8.7 billion languages
Located in brain port #7967200108, section 1.

An introduction of sorts

This book is an acting guide for all Overian envoys travelling to #7967200108, or 'Earth' as it's known to English-speaking natives of the planet.

First of all, congratulations on passing your entrance exam and successfully transporting to Earth. The suns are shining.

I make no apologies for using terms and a language unfamiliar to Overians; this is all part of the learning process.

As translator 2,019, I feel it is my honour and privilege to pass on some of my own acquired knowledge. I first arrived on Earth as part of the Millennium Convoy in the Earth-year 1983 (now known as the 'Berners-Lee batch').

1. Earthlings do not call themselves 'earthlings'. At this point in translation, earthlings are currently transitioning into

what they are calling 'globalisation'. It's a tricky adolescent stage – see the updated chapter seven, 'Growing pains and major setbacks', for more information.
2. 'Globe' is another English word for Earth. You will have learnt in training that there are around 6,000 spoken Earth languages. In English, alone, there are approximately 170,000 words in use – I recommend saving on brain space to only store around 9,000.
3. Earthlings believe it is the year 1994 AD – they have agreed collectively on 'Coordinated Universal Time', although no one can say why this is shortened to 'UTC' rather than 'CUT'.
4. Earthlings have, very recently, 'invented' the World Wide Web, with a huge helping hand from our native renegade Tim Berners-Lee – for more information, see Chapter 80, 'Why envoys should not intervene'. Earthlings are, at best, confused by the opportunities of a global information source. We continue to observe their progress.
5. At your own peril, eat a 'Doner kebab'.

Before we get down to the nitty-gritty, let's remind ourselves why we're all here. Nobody knows for sure, and never forget it.

> Your atoms have been transported over 1,000,000,000 Earth-miles to get here. If you're feeling strange, it would be odd if you weren't.

'Oh shut up,' screamed Polly into the cosmos, putting down the book on her side table. Why did that noise have to sound when she was utterly absorbed, not a moment ago, in the world of Overthere? She flung a dirty look at the bin, where her laptop merrily pinged, buzzed and bleeped away to itself. What would life be like without those lousy things? She wondered, would I be a different person? Would *I* be different? Who am *I* anyway? What makes me, *me*? Woah, big question.

She forced her eyes back to the book. It was a strange kind of book; she'd never looked at it properly before now. It was sandy to the touch; soft, yet it felt warm when sinking your fingers into it. It had the most beautiful aroma when opened. Polly had never visited a rainforest, but she assumed it smelt like the *Mentor Tome*. Now and then, Polly would be so distracted by the smell that she stopped reading and gave the book a good sniff. There was something else about the book too; when she held it, she felt calm. It felt too precious to read in a bad mood.

Picking the book up again, she continued to read.

> Your atoms have been transported over 1,000,000,000 Earth-miles to get here. If you're feeling strange, it would be odd if you weren't.

> How could I ever begin to describe to you what you are about to experience on Earth? I can't. For one of the smallest planets in our, thus far, discovered universe, it is deep, rich and hugely divided, in a way Overians have not experienced for thousands and thousands of years. Humans still die on this planet, and it is fascinating to see how this shapes their lives. Humans live to die, and every single interaction is based on this fate. In the mere 100 years that they have on the planet, almost all their thoughts, time and energy are focused on themselves. You may find that many humans barely even acknowledge you; do not be insulted, a good envoy is an undetected one.
>
> HI POLLY.

Polly blinked. Was the *Mentor Tome* talking to her? She looked back carefully; she could do without going mad. She already had a long-distance, alien boyfriend; it wouldn't take much.

> Yes, Polly, I am talking to you. I see you are not familiar with how a mentor tome works?

Polly looked around, then back at the words on the page in front of her.

> A mentor tome works in whatever way you choose it to work. You decided what you want it to say and do.

'If that's true then what was that first section about?' Polly spoke out-loud, feeling very self-conscious.

> You wanted to know about Overians and their experience of the Earth, didn't you?

The words continued to appear from nowhere in the little book.

Yes, thought Polly. This is weird.

> Well then that's what I gave you. I delivered it in a way that you would find most interesting.

'Are you real?' she asked in wonder.

> Good question. Yes and no.

Oh, thought Polly, another comedian, but out-loud asked, 'Can you read my thoughts?'

> How else could I respond to you? Yes, I can read your thoughts.

Uh oh, thought Polly, as an erect penis with a flag on it popped up in her mind, seemingly from nowhere.

'Are you a genie?'

> No. You have a bit of a thing about genies, you asked Donald if he was one several chapters ago.

So I did, remembered Polly. 'Talking of Donald, how do I get to Overthere?' She quickly cut to the nub of her worries.

> Are you sure you want to go? You might lose your mind or be forever lost. It's highly unlikely that you'll be able to come back to Earth and you'll be leaving your brother and all your friends behind.

The unknown wasn't scary and, as for losing her mind, well, the horse had already bolted on that one. Still, there was so much of Earth she hadn't seen. When she considered leaving it behind, it felt more precious to her than ever.

She thought of all her friends. She'd hardly seen Nic, Phil, Glenn or anyone for months. They'd understand, and, surely, they must have the internet on Overthere. As for Bert, she hadn't seen him for 10 years, so what would another 10 matter? What have I been doing these past 10 years? she wondered.

A pie chart appeared in the *Mentor Tome* entitled 'Polly Fairwold: time spent in the last 10 years'. It read:

> 47% sleeping
> 19% eating and cooking
> 12% working
> 11% thinking and making plans
> 10% in the pub
> 1% on the toilet

Polly found the summary of 10 years of life a little disappointing, but, on reflection, she was pleased with the results. She had loved it and would do it all again if she had the chance. What came next? More of the same? Too long she had spent inactive, directionless, held still.

She loved her friends dearly, knew that they would understand and that, somehow, she would see them again. But, in truth, she wasn't sure if she could actually come back.

> 'How likely is it that I will see my friends again?' she asked the *Mentor Tome*.

> Highly unlikely.

That isn't impossible, she thought hopefully.

> Almost impossible, unless you intend on living forever.

Who wants to live forever? wondered Polly. But before she could read the answer, the doorbell rang.

Chapter 20. Love codes life

> Nothing really matters,
> Anyone can see,
> Nothing really matters,
> Nothing really matters,
> To me.
>
> Queen, 'Bohemian Rhapsody', 1975.

'Now listen to me Ms Fairwold, I don't have a great deal of time.' Dr Matlock considered her doctor's appointment. 'For some unknown reason, and perhaps for no reason at all, you have managed to become crucial. Whatever you may think of me, I believe that you have a special purpose.' Dr Matlock looked her directly in her eyes.

'Do you want to come in and have a cup of tea? Oh no, wait, I don't have any milk,' interrupted Polly. The sight of Dr Matlock on her doorstep unnerved her.

'Please, be quiet and listen,' continued Dr Matlock, completely ignoring the offer. 'An opportunity is going to present itself. I don't know how, but you need to know something.' She paused, taking a deep breath. 'Change doesn't happen overnight, it takes small steps. When Overthere approached Earth, they had reasons. I believe they were able to understand that the Earth was in trouble, so intervened. Initially, nothing fundamentally changed. It took a long time to reach six-billion people. It took a long time for events to show their true impact. You have witnessed the opinions of people in high places, intelligent people that believe we must arm ourselves. Whatever your hapless, but no less dangerous, brother might think, Earth has no power to destroy Overthere. It has no idea where it even is. Overthere is safe from Earth, but Earth is not safe from herself.'

'What are you trying to tell me? I got lost at the bit about being quiet and listening,' confessed Polly.

'Earth is going to try to destroy itself.'

'Oh yes, I know that.' Polly twigged on.

'How do you know? Nevermind.' Dr Matlock checked her watch again. 'You need to follow your instinct. I don't know what you feel for Donald, but I am pretty sure he has an attachment to you. My advice is to consider *all* your options.'

'OK,' Polly said and nodded in, what she hoped looked like, a meaningful way.

'Good, so you understand. I have a great deal of work on my hands to divert people's attention. Your brother, unfortunately, is misguided in his efforts. He is right that Earth is lining up to attack Overthere, but he missed the most important point.'

Polly made a small noise.

'What is it?' Dr Matlock asked, irritated.

'You know when I said "OK", just now? Well, I think you might have read too much into it. What do you mean by *all* my options?' Polly asked.

'Oh, for heaven's sake. Only *you* can choose what comes next. I can't tell you what to do. Choose honestly, and you will choose wisely.' Dr Matlock turned to leave.

'Would one of those options involve travel?' asked Polly, desperate to know more.

'This isn't charades. OK, you tell me what options you have.' Dr Matlock folded her arms and tapped her foot in case it wasn't obvious enough she wanted to leave.

'Well, I could try and get Bert back.' Dr Matlock gave her a look that nearly took her skin off. 'No, well obviously I'm not going to do that,' said Polly quickly. 'I could go back to my job and just carry on, although I think I might have to find a new job.' Dr Matlock looked as frustrated as a chicken plopping out a tractor.

'Or I could...go after Donald?' Dr Matlock seemed to smile, or she would have done had she'd known how. It was less of a smile and more a non-angry face.

'But he's gone back to Overthere. How am I supposed to get there? Do you know how?'

'No, *I* don't. *You're* the one with the code. If that's what you want, I'm sure you can get there.' Dr Matlock again turned to leave.

'Can't you use it and help me?' Polly pleaded in a small voice.

'Don't be ridiculous. I can't use it. Can I trust you know what you need to do?'

'No,' said Polly despairingly, looking at her feet.

Polly had the feeling Dr Matlock was about to pat her on her head.

'Look, it's not easy to fall in love with someone that lives on another planet. It's especially difficult when that someone is the only chance the Earth has to empower itself. It doesn't have to be an unhappy ending, you know. You get to decide.' Dr Matlock's voice softened.

'Can I talk to Bert?' Polly looked up at her with sad eyes.

'OK, you can call him. I'll give you two minutes.' Dr Matlock handed over a piece of paper with a number on it.

'Call in 10 minutes. I'll need to sanction it first,' agreed Dr Matlock.

'OK,' said Polly.

'What?' Dr Matlock had already started to march off. She stopped and gave Polly a death stare.

'You seemed to know what you're talking about back there, with that being in love thing.' Polly felt like she prodded a poisonous snake.

Dr Matlock suddenly smiled; she was an astonishingly attractive woman. 'Yes. Falling for someone unavailable might seem like the hardest pain, but it can be what ultimately sets you free. Free from thinking one type of love is the only interesting thing worth pursuing in life. Belief in "the one" has certainly kept a lot of highly influential pioneers at bay.' She flicked her nails. 'Perhaps I am not the best person to advise you about matters of the heart. There's as much evidence to prove that belief in the one is powerful enough to help you travel to the edge of the universe and back. But, as I keep telling you, what you want to believe is your choice.'

'Perhaps both are true,' pondered Polly.

'Ah, now you're talking. I think we're going to be OK, don't you Polly?' nodded Dr Matlock.

Polly nodded back.

'Thank you,' Polly mumbled. A non-angry look appeared on Dr Matlock's face again.

'It was *nothing*,' she said, turned and left.

Chapter 21. Polly goes to Overthere

> It's tiring reaching out for something just out of reach, but I'll get it.
> After all, what I want isn't as easy as all that.
>
> Public Service Broadcast, 'Inform – Educate – Entertain', 2013.

Polly dialled the number for Bert and waited for the line to connect. It was a dead tone. She hung up and paced around her flat, picking up objects in the blind hope that something would inspire an answer.

In Polly's life, stuff just happened. She never gave anything much thought and explained away everything using spirited little sayings such as: 'You can't win them all', 'Better than to have loved and lost than to have never loved at all' and 'Live your life in the sunshine'. She would say them to herself and others, these little mantras; none of them mean much to her, yet they brought comfort.

In later years, Polly had faced monstrous demons and all manner of fears. She had suffered pain from the depths of her soul, yet sometimes thought she'd take that over the pain of standing on an upturned plug or stubbing her toe.

When she thought about it, life was an incredibly sweet and lovely pastime. She would bask in its glorious sunshine for as long as it would allow.

Sprawled out on a comfy sofa surrounded by books, Polly had one hand tucked between her thighs and a cup of tea in the other.

People have wrestled with the mystery of why the universe exists for thousands of years. Every Earth culture came up with its own creation story – most of them leaving the matter in the hands of the gods – and philosophers have had a lot to say on the subject.

However, in recent years, physicists and cosmologists have started to take the question a bit more seriously. They point out that we now have an understanding of the history of the universe, as well as the physical laws that describe how it works. That information, they say, should give us a clue about how and why the cosmos exists.

They answer that the entire universe – from the fireball of the Big Bang to the star-studded jacket in Polly's wardrobe – popped into existence from nothing at all. It had to happen, they say, because 'nothing' is inherently unstable.

This idea may sound bizarre, or just another fanciful creation story. But the physicists argue that it follows naturally from science's two most potent and successful theories: quantum mechanics and general relativity.

Here, then, is how everything could have come from nothing.

SNAP

'What the hell was that?' Polly jumped up from the sofa. She looked around her, but there was no apparent culprit. A new thought, however, had popped into Polly's head.

Donald had transported himself somehow, and he needed the *Mentor Tome* to do it. No wait, that wasn't true, it was something else. He had been singing something.

It might sound crazy, but she was going to try it anyway – she would lie in bed, listen to music and read the *Mentor Tome*.

She opened the piece of paper that was handed to her by Donald on their first encounter. She looked at it and, holding the *Mentor Tome*, asked – how do I get to Overthere?
Slowly she lifted it to her face to read.

> We end this particular ending, with everything.
> Everything to dream for.
> Good night, sweet dreams Polly.

Chapter 22. Tony cleans up

A black cab pulled up outside the large and unimpressive Landmark Hotel. Donald Pigeon, having spent the last three days in the bath, had finally ventured out into the open and hailed a cab. Tony watched with a mildly amused gaze, as the long-legged beanpole of a man leapt into the available car ahead. Scratching his upper lip, Tony wondered if it was time to retire. It had been a slow week, following a slow month, following a slow year; he thought it might be time to pack it all in. If only June would see sense and agree to move to Cyprus for their twilight years. He could envision himself now, cocktail in hand, sun high in the sky, desert heat warming his tubby body. June said she wanted to move to Padstow and, as much as he enjoyed the odd excursion to the rocky coast on the tip of the British isles, he didn't much relish the thought of the winter months down there – catching a cold and having fish and chips for dinner every night. Tony thought of himself as more of a halloumi man.

While Tony basked in his exotic daydream, a large, red-bearded man exited the hotel and made for the cab. With him, the most unusual female with a very tidy mane of silver-blonde hair and an immaculately set face.

Red beard opened the cab door, making Tony jump up in his seat a little.

'Where to mate?' Tony's deep, jolly voice returning to him.

'Putney,' came the gruff reply, with not the nearest hint of lightness.

Tony was good at his job. He knew people, and people liked him in general. He also knew when to keep his mouth shut. Tony pulled away disappointed, as it was unlikely this man and the spectacular lady were going to talk much. The eyes of the woman flashed him a look of disdain in the cab mirror. Tony firmly looked forward and switched on the privacy button to let them get on with it. Tony almost felt sorry for the bloke with the red beard; he knew a row when one was coming.

By accident, his privacy button flicked back to 'off'.

'It's not my fault Janet. No one could have predicted what happened,' the red-bearded man pleaded with her. 'I don't know how we get her back and all our spies tell us has left the planet. We have to get back to Overthere sooner rather than later. We must help her. Polly has no idea what she's doing.' The red-bearded man sounded desperate.

'Well she soon will,' Janet responded, flicking her hair. 'And if Donald thinks he can get away with what he's done, innocent or not, he's in for it,' she growled.

'It's not his fault, is it?' red beard replied.

'We'll see. I hope not. I hope he's not that stupid.' Janet folded her arms in a matter-of-fact kind of way.

'Why, what's going to happen? Can you see it? Can you see the future? Where are we going?' Red beard shook her by the arm.

'I don't know, but I promise it's not going to be boring,' Janet said, smirking.

Interesting thought Tony, flipping back the privacy switch.

Very interesting indeed.

Printed in Great Britain
by Amazon